THE TUMOR'S NAME WAS HERALD

ONE PERSON'S JOURNEY OF INITIATION

Paula Payne Hardin, EdD, MPS

ISBN   978-1-966473-29-9 Ebook
ISBN   978-1-966473-28-2 Paperback

The EC Publishing LLC books may be ordered
through booksellers or by contacting:

EC Publishing LLC
116 South Magnolia Ave.
Suite 3, Unit F
Ocala, FL 34471, USA
Direct Line: +1 (352) 644-6538
Fax: +1 (800) 483-1813
http://www.ecpublishingllc.com/

Ordering Information:
Quantity sales. Special discounts are available on quantity purchases by corporations, associations, and others. For details, contact the publisher at the address above.

Printed in the United States of America

TABLE OF CONTENTS

INTRODUCTION

On April 14, 2000, I learned I had cancer, colorectal cancer. Such a humble part of the body, the rectum. Certainly a part I paid as little attention to as possible. Yet it became the site for an amazing meeting with the Divine, the Great Friend. I came to call my discovery of cancer and all that followed an 'Initiation.' In this Initiation, I connected to a luminous Force or Being of astonishing love and enchanting humor.

The following pages come from my heart. Actually much of the writing is quoted from my journal. In the beginning I wrote for my own healing, wanting to better understand what was happening to me. Now I write to reach out to others who are entering initiations of whatever kind. I have a message of hope. Don't be afraid. All the events of our lives come from Love. They come to show us the way to happiness, the way to heal from suffering.

The drawings come from my heart as well. They come out of my search for meaning. I drew so I could understand my illness and turn all that was happening into an affirmation of life. I drew from some happy, truthful Source in me. Obviously I have no technical expertise. I am a beginner wanting to express something beyond words. I call my images 'soul drawings.'

I did not draw or write with publishing in mind. That thought evolved when people (family, medical personnel, friends, chaplains, etc.) urged me to write a short, simple book sharing my journey and my drawings.

So, blessings to you, dear reader. Sometimes we stumble under the load when there is no one to show us a better way. We fall when there is no one who knocks on our heart's door offering to walk with us. My hope is that you will allow me to walk with you through these pages. I wish for you that you learn more about the astonishing Light of your own being and that you will want to share that Light with others.

Paula
At the farm
August, 2000

CHAPTER ONE

A JOURNEY BEGINS

For years and years I struggled
Just to love my life. And then
the butterfly
rose, weightless, on the wind,
"Don't love your life too much," it said.

And vanished
into the world.

Mary Oliver

Learn to love your life! Don't love your life too much! It can all be so confusing. Round and round my mind can go... love your life, don't love your life too much, where's the balance, what's right? I guess I'll leave questions like these to the philosophers. Yet, this much I have found to be true; the answer to living this life is to live the life that is coming to me without resistance, accepting everything, I mean everything, as necessary and full of lessons and gifts. As the ancient philosopher Lao Tsu said: "So to yield to life is to solve the unsolvable."

Yesterday, April 14, 2000, I received the news from dear Dr. Sangchant at the end of a colonoscopy procedure that I had colon/rectal cancer. Groggy from the anesthetic, the Doctor's words echoed off the walls of my not too sharp mind "you have cancer…. you have cancer…." The first thing my mind responded with is: "I don't see myself with cancer, I don't have the cancer personality…."

I don't know where that piece of information came from, but somewhere in my brain was tucked a study describing the type of person likely to get cancer. I vaguely remember some kind of a simple questionnaire claiming it could tell me whether I was the type to get cancer or not. I took the "test" answering questions like "Do you keep your feelings to yourself?" "Do you try to please others even if you end up not doing what you want to do?" "Do people take advantage of you?" "Are you living the life you want?"

Needless to say, I was not an unbiased responder, how can one answer yes to questions you know will eventually tell you are the type to get cancer? However, type or not, the good Doctor finds cancer and that is a fact. I have a tumor growing in my lower colon.

The colonoscopy is completed and pictures of the tumor taken. I am back in my clothes sipping hot tea the attentive nurse brought. My friend Jackie Rivet-River is coming to drive me home. Still a bit light-headed I now understand why I was warned not to drive after the procedure.

"How are you doing?" Jackie asks. "I have cancer, I wonder what I am supposed to learn…" I respond. "This is a shock to me, Jackie, I have never seen myself as having the 'cancer personality.'"

THE FIRST THING I DO

The very first thing I do when I get home and my head clears is to get on the phone and call people who love me and whom I love. I ask, unashamedly, for their help, their support and prayers during this time. It makes no difference to me what their religion or lack of is: Jewish, Catholic, Fundamentalist, Atheist, Buddhist, Earth based, whatever! Good will and good thoughts carry an energy that reaches out and blesses both those who send and those who receive. In my heart I have felt this to be true and now there is research; amazing studies confirm that positive, loving thoughts promote healing and growth in people, animals and plants.

THE FIRST NIGHT

I sleep well. The calm that came when I first heard I had cancer stays with me. I am a bit amazed at myself. But as a gray morning comes and with it a gentle spring rain, some thoughts intrude: what if this condition proves fatal, how will I deal with it? Then: what will I do with my dear cats, who will love them and take them? And my little fish family, who will care for them?

Then I begin thinking of who I can count on to help me if I become helpless. As an older, single woman (age 66) with adult children who live far away, I wonder what arrangements I ought to make.

"DON'T GO THERE!"

The message comes loud and clear: *Don't go there. It's too soon. You don't have enough data. Stay in the moment. Trust my love and trust that what you need and want will be there for you when you need and want it!"*

This was the first of a number of "messages" I receive during what I have come to call my Initiation process. I see my cancer as an important Initiation, an Initiation into profound spiritual truths, emotional healing, a new appreciation of my body and new strengths. How did the messages come? Mostly just a strong thought in my mind. Sometimes they came as I wrote in my journal.

I have been a spiritual seeker for many years. Meditation, journaling, dream work, studies and different therapies have been aids on my path. I feel fortunate that I have these skills and tools to use during this crisis. Recently I have moved beyond being a seeker, to becoming a finder as well.

DAY 5 OF MY INITIATION, I FEEL SUPPORTED

How do I feel this 5th day of my initiation after the news about my cancer? Well for one thing, I feel I am receiving a lot of attention. I feel support from friends and family as well as from inner allies (for example I have a guardian angel named Magenta who is so caring). I begin to make a list of those who offer to care for me, do research for me, accompany me for tests or to the hospital.

A message comes that influences me deeply: *"You are so right about seeing this experience as an initiation, a time of opportunity. It is not your time to go. You have a Jot of living and giving ahead.*

"I know part of you would like to Jay this life down, but it is not your time. You are in a time of reaping rewards and giving birth to your new way of teaching. Joy is coming to you and there is a greater fullness of joy opening to you. Dear heart, this time won't even be hard. You will be guided each step along the way.

"This event of yours is having an effect on all around you. As your friends say you have given so much and now it is time for them to give to you. You are to receive now, hear? You have been taken for granted in some ways, now that is over. You are to absorb in the cells of your deepest core that you are loved and lovable. Loved and lovable!"

I REALIZE THREE GUIDES HAD COME TO PREPARE ME

A few months before all this in late December 1999, I was browsing at a Barnes and Noble bookstore when a couple of books just jumped from the shelf and into my arms. Have you ever had that experience? It's really quite astonishing how it happens! One was the book *Friendship with God* by Neale Donald Walsch and the other was *The Path of Love*, poems by Jelaluddin Rumi, a 13th century Sufi mystic.

The Walsch book heralded a transition for me. I have always had difficulty with the word 'God.' It carries too much baggage of a harsh judgmental all-powerful male who sends people to hell when they displease him. I was taught he also required the death of his son in order to be satisfied. Well, all this was just too much for a sensitive little girl. For years I hardly knew what to do with my deeply spiritual nature.

As I matured, the words Great Spirit were acceptable. Creative Force, Divine Being, all worked—sort of. But with the Walsch book, I begin to think in terms of a friendship with this great force. Friend is a word that carries no baggage for me.

I remember well when I read a comment by Einstein. He was asked "What is the most important question in life?" His response was: "Is it a friendly universe?" Well, is it? I had learned to answer this question with a tentative yes. Now my thinking was taken to a new place. If it is a friendly universe, then there must be a friend, or friends who created this vast universe.

Walsch wrote convincingly about a friendship with God, and my heart was ready to hear this message. Yes, I could accept the word Friend as a substitute term for God, the Friend, the Great Friend!

And so my heart opened to a profound friendship with a profound Force, whatever that might mean. How could I learn more about this new Friend? Perhaps nature was one of the best ways since I felt the Friend was also Creator. So, with increased attention, I began to ponder nature as revealer of the Great Friend's essence.

A WONDROUS COMMUNICATION

It is the morning of December 30 and I am at my little farm house in northwest Indiana, away from city noise and lights. Rising while still dark I go out in the crisp winter air. Hugging my robe about me I note the silvery moon's slim cradle in the lightening sky and the abundance of stars everywhere. All is silent, I feel a rich reverence pervading the moment.

Suddenly through the sky a falling star comes shooting directly toward me. I am stunned. A falling star in a December sky? I've never heard of such a thing. I feel it a sign of communication, a wink from a Friend so vast and wondrous that it can throw a star across the morning sky to announce that I have a Friend in the Beyond.

I am at risk here, personalizing a natural phenomenon, but it was so special. I was only out for a few moments and I saw it. Somewhere deep inside I feel acknowledged as I grope toward friendship with the Great Friend. This leads me to give another name to the Friend, "Star-Thrower."

STAR-THROWER SPEAKS

The next morning during my meditation time, I decide to open the other book that had "jumped" into my arms while I was at the bookstore. This one is a beautifully boxed combination of 50 illustrated cards with a poem by Rumi on each, accompanied by a little book of explanations and interpretations. With a sense of anticipation, I break through the plastic wrap and open the box. The card pack is wrapped separately. As I begin opening it I notice that the deck begins with #3. Oh my, I wonder, did they forget #1 and 2? Or are the cards just mixed up because the sorting machine got mixed up?

Anyway, being the orderly type, I begin to sort the cards arranging them in sequence from #1-#50. Suddenly the thought comes to me, why not look at #3, after all, some trouble was taken to make sure that card was on top of the deck—see what it says. So I did. And here's what came to me.

> Oh lovers, lovers, it is time
> to set out from the world
> I hear a drum in my soul's ear
> coming from the depths of the stars.

Floodgates of desire open in me, desire to know the Drummer who sends messages from the depths of the stars. Desire to explore a relationship with 'Star-Thrower,' the Great Friend. I feel a sense of awe growing. What a possibility—to have access to a Being so far greater, so beyond, so big and mysterious that someone like me can not even get my head around it.

Then fear grips my heart, am I being sophomoric here? Am I regressing into a naive former stage in my life when I cried out over and over to know and understand the Great One? When I prayed and prayed to a silent, dismal, punishing god and there was no answer? How can I let go of some of those deep feelings of disappointment and betrayal with religion, with God?

At that moment a message came:
Don't go there! Don't judge yourself! You were a soul trying to find her way back home. You were lost, confused, making mistakes and seeking all the while. Honor that person you were. You are who you are now because you stand on the shoulders of her experience. Indeed, embrace and thank her for all she went through without giving up. It will all make sense to you one day. You are almost at

the place where you can be deeply grateful for yourself and your life. You will soon appreciate it all and the magical journey it truly has been.

I accept this message and return to the poem. There is today a reaching out to me from the depth of the stars, traveling like a drum-beat across space. The Great Sound, the Sound that can only be heard in the depths of my soul, with the ears of my soul.

About the same time my dear friend, Titia Ellis, sent me a book of poems by Hafiz *I Heard God Laughing.* She inscribed the book: "For Paula, a way to be with 'The Friend.'" Although I was mesmerized by the poetry from the beginning, neither of us knew just how powerful these poems would become for me.

WHAT DOES IT MEAN?

OK, I wrote in my journal on January 2, 2000, what does having a relationship with a Great Friend like you mean? Response:

1) *It means knowing—really knowing—that you are safe, beloved, never alone. REALLY KNOWING.*
2) *It means you can ask me all questions and I will respond- all questions!*
3) *It means having great wisdom available to you.*
4) *It means gifts of strength, courage, peace, and insight infusing you all the time.*
5) *I will introduce you to incredible people to be with on this soul journey.*
6) *It means knowing what you are to do and loving doing it because you understand more fully what you Jove to do.*
7) *It means sensing just how great you really are and Jetting that sense grow and grow so that you begin to act like the great friend to me that you truly are.*
8) *It means taking all boundaries, all constraints off your heart and mind because you now are so safe, your needs met so fully, you can be free! Liberated! Joyous! Boundless! There is no eternal punishment. There is no mistake so great it can't be touched with healing.*
9) *It means a feeling of completion, and profound health at your heart's core.*
10) *You now welcome challenges because they are gateways to the promised land.*
11) *You welcome changes because they bring a richer and fuller sense of who you truly are.*
12) *You, as master of your life, now lead others in their journey to mastery, because we are Friends.*

And so my relationship with the Great Friend deepens and joy fills the air I breath. My heart is coming home from a long, long journey. Home. Whenever I try to speak of my experiences with Star-Thrower the Great Friend, tears well up.

Something important is happening within me. I know I am being touched by something great. Little did I know I was being prepared for one of the most profound initiations of my life. Looking back, my heart is awed by the timing. Some Master Planner was guiding me, making sure all the arrangements were in place for what needed to come—down to the smallest detail.

DAY 6 OF MY INITIATION, I BEGIN A NEW PROJECT

Now, my story returns to April. I told you about finding the Great Friend a few months ago because I want you to sense how I have been prepared in a most loving way for this cancer Initiation.

A new hunger comes to me during this time—a hunger to express myself with images and colored pens. Words are OK, but there is something wonderful about images and colors. I begin on my lined paper in my journal. I am obsessed with stars. More and more stars begin to fill the almost daily journal writings, colorful, different sizes and shapes. The star that represents Star-Thrower is always large and has a sparkling path behind it. I go to a store and buy some heavier paper and more colored pens.

On Day 6, April 20, I feel the urge to draw a female figure, it is supposed to be me, but she looks so young and I don't know how to make her look more my age. It is my first drawing of a human form beyond a stick figure. You can see in the picture that I think the tumor is higher up than it really is. Nevertheless, I know that the picture title is "Initiation." This is Drawing 1.

Then I want to draw my spirit body, this I title 'Opportunity' and this becomes Drawing 2. With these two 'soul drawings' a series began that unfolded as my cancer Initiation unfolded.

A word about what I mean by 'soul drawings.' I want to express something deep and essential with images and color but I recognize that I am not a skilled artist, proficient in techniques. So I coin the term 'soul drawings' to free me from feeling I have to draw well. Besides they do carry soul for me.

I've since talked to people who are part of what they call 'self taught' art groups. They assure me that I am not alone in wanting to express myself artistically. Many are expressing themselves from their creative source and, like me, do not want to feel pushed into lessons and prescribed forms.

DAY 7 OF MY INITIATION, THE TUMOR BECOMES REAL

It is April 21 and I am returning to the city from the farm. I have a number of appointments to keep. The first is with Dr. Martha Howard, an MD who runs Wellness Associates in Chicago. Dr. Howard and her associates blend both western and eastern medicine in their holistic approach to health.

Initiation
Day 6
April 20 '00

opportunity

Day 6
April 20, '00

2.

Dr. Howard comes into the room where the receptionist placed me. She sits on a swivel chair, pad and pen in hand, and looks at me: "I received Dr. Sangchant's reports on your cancer." Then I learn that my medical challenge is to save my rectum. Since the tumor is placed so low there might not be enough healthy tissue to surgically reconnect the bowel once the diseased tissue is removed. The usual treatment in cases like mine is to prepare a patient for a life-long colostomy. Well I can live with that, but it would not be my first choice!

Martha continues "We have to make a plan!" So we put together a program of cleansing herbs, weekly sessions, acupuncture, etc. The goal is to prepare me for the rigorous medical interventions that are sure to come.

"Now, Paula, we need to uncover the belief system that allowed this to happen. Do you have any thoughts on that?"

"Well," I began, "The journey of grief over my son's addiction has, I'm sure, diminished my immune system. I have been unable to sleep much for months as his marriage collapsed and his business went downhill. The situation has gone on for so long and I tried too hard to help. My health deteriorated with the stress until I realized I was putting myself at risk. I realized that there was nothing I could do anymore."

"I'm free now. He's out of my life. I pray for him, but I don't accept calls or see him. Now I have healed enough to be able to sleep. My mind has stopped whirling and I'm not depressed anymore. In fact the pain of my grief had me in its clutches like a giant wave. The wave has gone back out to sea now, leaving treasures on the beach, treasures of gratitude for life, peace, acceptance and more. You already know about the father wound I've had and its profound influence on my life and relationships…."

"Paula, when children have had abusive homes like you and I had, it is often hard for them to ever trust, particularly a man. We must find out what the tumor has come to say. Have you talked to your tumor?"

"No, I haven't thought of that, but I will."

"Let's be silent right now and listen to what it might have to say…"

We closed our eyes, breathed deeply 3 times and waited.

"I hear it say that it is afraid that we want to get rid of it." Martha broke the silence.

I took that in and then said: "Well, I have been working on healing images I can use. I don't like the war ones that some use. I don't like the language of killing—even a tumor. So far I haven't come up with a healing image that feels just right.

"Paula, talk to the tumor."

"Mr. Tumor (I suddenly realize the tumor is masculine), let's make a plan together that we can both agree on. Maybe we can both get our needs met in a win-win situation. On one hand, if you keep on, I'll die and then you'll die too. If I have radiation and chemotherapy, you'll have a tough time. If I have surgery, they'll take you out and put you on a junk heap. So we have to make a plan."

Martha interrupted, "Paula, don't open your eyes, take my hand, move to this chair. Now, you become the tumor and respond.

"I don't want to go. I like it here. It's warm and squishy, just like I like it. But you have a point, now that you know I'm here, everything has changed. My future is in jeopardy. I'll consider a plan..."

Me, back in the other chair: "Well, the angel helper beings could begin creating new cells, putting them in the bowel wall underneath you as you release to go to your new destiny. Would that work?"

Martha: "Good work! Great! This is a beginning. Now we must expand the plan and strengthen the images!"

FEELING GOOD

I left feeling good; I have the beginnings of a plan and some good information to go on. I also have a wonderful doctor to be on my team. I am ready to begin a regimen of herbs and immune system support, plus a series of acupuncture treatments.

I fo home, get my mail and listen to my messages. There was my son's voice after a month; "Hi Mom, are you going to talk to me yet? I need some money...." I fast forward and erase the message. I realize this manis not to be in my life at this time. I am stronger in my resolve. He needs to find out who he is, deal with his life and his choices. I must not sacrifice my life on the altar of misguided motherhood to a grown man of 39 years.

MY NAME IS HERALD

Later I think of my time with Dr. Howard and the conversation with the tumor. Then I wonder, should the tumor have a name? No, I'm not going to personalize this thing! That's going too far. It's a bit way out to be having conversations with it, that's enough!

I turn to leave the room when a voice in my head says clearly "My name is Herald as in 'Hark the Herald Angels Sing!,,, Oh my God! What was that? OK, Herald it is. Herald the messenger.

CHAPTER TWO

MY LIFE IS TURNED UP-SIDE-DOWN

I wish I could show you,
When you are lonely or in darkness
The astonishing Light
Of your own Being!

Hafiz

INITIATION DAY 8, HERALD BEGINS TO HELP

The next day, Day 8 of my Initiation, I am back at the farm. Rising early I do a drawing of an image representing my bowel. I place Herald more accurately, very low. I see tiny angels bringing healthy cells to line the wall and prevent the tumor from pushing on through and metastasizing, this I label Drawing 3. I begin to see Herald as letting go. But I still don't have an image of where Herald will go so his needs will be met as well as mine.

There are big life-style changes. I extend my sabbatical from work. Pills and herbs fill the refrigerator and I arrange them in little dishes for the different times I need to take them during the day. A new juicer sits on my counter and the frig is stocked with veggie leaves, green, the darker the better. I am to drink fresh green veggie juice 2X's a day. My days revolve around my health and boosting my immune system through rest, nourishing food, exercise, herbs and meditation. The phone rings more than usual and I am surprised and touched by people's concern.

Miracles are becoming commonplace. For example I didn't yet know who my medical team would be. I knew I needed to begin to research this. Then a miracle happens.

3. Harold is beginning to let go.
Angels lining healthy cells to line the
bowel wall. 4-22-00

It's morning and I have volunteered for 'goat duty,' so I go out to feed the cute little goats, a task I love. I spot my neighbors, Maureen and Tom Fuechtmann, out for a walk on the lawn near the big white barn. Going over for a visit I mention my cancer diagnosis. Maureen, who heads up the chaplain's program at Loyola University Medical Center, becomes very assertive as this is her world. "Paula, you must put yourself in the hands of a big teaching hospital immediately. I have the name of a doctor whom I would trust with my life. She will organize your whole team. I will call her first thing Monday morning and tell her to expect your call. You must act quickly!"

The name of the doctor Maureen mentions is one my good friend Marianne Johnson uses, Dr. Fran Langdon. Now that is serendipity! I had been wishing Marianne was around because she is so knowledgeable about the medical system, having worked as a nurse for many years before she became a psychotherapist. But she and her husband, Bill, (who had been in the navy and loves all ships and boats) are sailing in some far off place and I haven't been able to contact them for weeks. Dr. Fran Langdon. I remember meeting her when Marianne had surgery last year and I helped as I could.

INITIATION DAY 9, A CT SCAN MADE FUN

Early the next morning, Easter, April 23, I head for the city and St. Joseph Hospital because I have a CT scan. My appointment was rescheduled to Easter because the scanning equipment broke down last week. I didn't mind because, I reason, Easter is a good day for resurrections. The hospital is as empty and quiet as Jesus' tomb! My friend Jackie promised to stop by for a few minutes before going to church, but she surprises me by being in the lobby when I arrive. In her hand is an Easter basket full of treats.

I am   given a quart of something that looks and has the consistency of Elmer's glue to drink—not bad really. Soon the door to the 'drinking' room opens and my dear friend, Patti Slama, comes in. I am so surprised! She and Jackie had arranged it all. I am touched that people would leave their families on Easter to come and wait here with me.

We get to laughing as I tell my friends that the tumor is male and has a name which he informed me was Herald as in 'Hark the Herald Angels Sing.' Jackie thinks that since the tumor is male, we have to think of his ego in making a win-win plan. If it was female, she would, of course, give her life to help another, but Herald might need to be made to feel important! Perhaps he could have his name go down in history for a medical breakthrough—the first talking tumor. By now we are giddy with laughter. Then I drink another quart of goo. This one was a bit harder to get down but friends make the process easier!

Shortly after this experience, I do Drawing 4, the angel parade with Herald leading. I have never drawn feet before, so this is a challenge. Hands are still finger-less! No noses on the faces, but my soul is nourished as I express myself and I am having fun.

INITIATION DAY 10, GETTING A MEDICAL TEAM TOGETHER

My step-daughter, Nancy, comes for a couple days. She has taken my news hard having lost both her mother and her father as well as a number of other important people. So much illness and death in her young life. She comes bringing me thoughtful gifts. I am touched. We know we can count on each other when we need to.

I don't have much time to spend with her as I must contact Dr. Langdon, the internist who Maureen recommended. Then following Dr. Langdon's directions I contact the colorectal surgeon (how do you like that word, colorectal? I had never heard it before, it is someone who specializes in colon and rectal surgery). I also contact the radiation-oncology doctor and the hematology-oncology doctor.

Oh my, so much to learn and keep track of. I need a way to organize the material so I buy a three-ring notebook in a color that appeals. I get dividers and label one for each doctor; one for the herbal program I'm on; one to keep track of medications; another to keep track of the alternative therapies I use and so on. On the first page I scotch tape all the professional cards of my team with their addresses and phone numbers.

THE MEDICAL SYSTEM IS DIFFICULT AT FIRST

I found the medical system difficult to break into. I realize I was a bit timid at first about pushing my agenda when everyone seemed so busy and even brusque and I was just another faceless name with a problem.

It took about three days of continuous phone time to put a plan, complete with appointments, in place. The phones were often busy or I was put on hold for long periods. I left messages but my calls weren't returned or I couldn't get past the receptionist who said "I'm sorry we don't have an opening for you for another 6 weeks." "But, this is an emergency and I can't wait 6 weeks." "I'm sorry, but there are no openings."

I finally learn to go a round the system. I call the referring doctor and ask her or him to get me an appointment and guess what... I can get in the very next day!

SAVE A RECTUM!
SAVE A RECTUM!
SAVE A RECTUM!
I'll help save a rectum!
Herald takes his place at the front of the parade

Once I learn how to manage the system, I find it to be filled with knowledgeable, hard working, kind people, but it took some effort. I wonder how others manage, those who have English as a second language, or those really feeling sick or who are old and feeble. It is difficult for me and I feel energetic, besides I am used to dealing with systems and institutions.

In the middle of all these arrangements I receive this message while writing in my journal. The message begins like a letter. The salutation evolved after I began calling the Friend 'Star-Thrower.'

Dear Star-Seer,

Go on and write, don't be afraid that you aren't hearing my voice. Just trust and keep on keeping on!

You are on a gift-filled path. Keep your eyes open and enjoy. Remember I promised this time wouldn't be hard. Has it been hard yet?

Remember one of the things you are to learn, you are lovable, people Jove you, you are not alone in all this. The blessings will keep rolling in.

Love, your Friend Star-Thrower

INITIATION DAY 13, HERALD AS KILLER

I have a friend, Annette Houlefeld, who is something of a sage or shaman. I decide to make an appointment with her and take a 'shamanic journey.' I seek understanding of the deeper dynamics of my cancer. Annette uses drums and chanting to access other realms of consciousness. There she meets guides, asks questions and receives information for her client. My task is to lie down and let the drumming and chanting bless me.

Annette said that Jesus came this time along with Mary Magdalene. He said that what is happening to me is part of an evolutionary process. Yes it is my journey but it is symbolic of what needs to happen in the larger world.

As there has been violence between men and women in my life, so it is in the world. These ancient angers are keeping us from our next step as humans. I must surrender to the process going on in my body and I will be protected, healed. In his base form, Herald is a killer. When I get radiation, imagine the fire of God going through me, transmuting the killer rage and going out in a release of new, higher energy. This will help Herald transform into a more evolved state. I leave Annette's house with much to ponder.

THE MESSAGE OF NOW

Interesting that I never asked 'why me?' because, why not me? Should I be spared when all around sisters and brothers are enduring trials of every sort? I'm glad 'why? doesn't plague me. I truly resonate with Lao Tsu: "So to yield to life is to solve the unsolvable."

I do struggle with having my mind pulled into the past, my regrets, my wishes that I had been wiser, done things differently, or things had turned out differently. Ohhh the past, it keeps tugging, slurping, pulling.

Then when I look ahead, all the medical procedures, the operations, the radiation and chemotherapy, I get scared, my heart races, my mind goes out of control with the 'what ifs.' I must stay in this moment, take a deep breath and harness my mind to focus on now. As soon as I honor the present moment, all unrest and struggle dissipate and I become aware of the beauty about me, the kindness on every hand, the wonder and gift of life itself!

Dear Star-Thrower, have you a message for me?

Dear Star-Seer,

My messages to you have been constant. You are pluming the secrets of this cancer initiation. "NOW" Is surely a main one. Living in the now.

Look at what has happened this week! You have a top surgeon and the two of you really clicked! He is in your corner. People are coming from everywhere to support you, both in the seen and unseen realms. Miracles will continue to attend you, keep alert.

Just think how early you detected and acted on this cancer and the good people who have appeared to work on your behalf.

Don't look back, that is all in my hands, don't look forward, that's in my hands too. Just be with me now in the present.

Your Friend

After this message, I began Drawing 6, but put it aside because I was having difficulty trying to express what I felt. Simplicity is the key for my drawings, and this one kept becoming too confusing and complicated. The minute struggle enters in, I know to stop. Perhaps there is more I need to learn before I can continue.

INITIATION DAY 18, MY HEAD IS TURNED AROUND

A friend, Betty Rothenberger, told me of her friend, Deborah Light, a clergy in the Covenant of the Goddess, who had cancer. She has a more severe diagnosis than mine but it has been in remission now for some time. Deborah, Betty told me, used some images for her healing that created a lasting impression on Betty and since I was still working with what images I might use for my process, she felt I might benefit from a conversation with Deborah. Betty warned me that Deborah was a very busy woman and might be difficult to contact, but not to give up.

I dial the number Betty gave me and guess who answers the phone? Yes, Deborah. She gives generously of herself and her time and she profoundly influences my whole process by helping me 're-frame' my experience. I take notes on our conversation so I won't miss a thing. She understands completely my desire to avoid all war-like images and words, all concepts about killing the tumor and fighting the disease. I know there is a more peaceful way and I want to find it, a way in which all parties involved gain something.

I told her of my impression that the tumor has a name (Herald as in "Hark the Herald Angels Sing") and the way that name came to me. She didn't seem to think me weird and ready to be carted away by those fellas in the white coats!

Regarding Herald, here are some of Deborah's insights as I remember them: "Herald exists. It is unfair not to consider his prana, his essence. All matter is holy. His essence is telling you to 'Hark!' 'Listen!' He came to you as a tumor, what is his message? From where did he come?

"In his present form, he is a killer. So, looking at where Herald is in your body, you need to face that there is a murderous rage in you that you want to expel. Herald is like the fallen angel, Lucifer, in the Biblical story of how the devil came to be. Lucifer, before his fall, was one of the high angels on a level with Michael and Gabriel. He was a fire bringer, a light bringer, but something happened and he fell into becoming the devil.

"See your process as a transformation of rage. Begin to see your tumor as a hot flame that transforms into cooling waters, becoming a nourishing mist or vapor that goes forth greening the countryside like it does in Ireland, the Emerald Isle."

CREATING SACRED RITUAL

Deborah continues, now suggesting ways for me to create a sacred ritual out of my process of hospital visits and doctors appointments; of chemotherapy and radiation that is sure to come.

"Before you go to treatments, select something special to wear, something you really like and feel good in. You are going to the 'Temple of Healing' (I was jolted by that one, changing the image of the hospital to the Temple of Healing, but it felt right). This is a holy and ceremonious event, so adorn yourself, wear something beautiful, at least a lovely scarf! Think of the doctors and other trained personnel as ministers and priests in the Temple of Healing. They train for years just to be able to be agents of healing. Consider these things.

"As the chemo is going into your veins, remember that all chemicals came from the earth, from the Goddess. Think of all those that did the research to discover the healing qualities of chemotherapy and that the research was done with high motivation—to help people heal.

"When you are in radiation, the rays will come into your body to do what they were meant to do, heal you. You will be alone in that room for the treatment and you must do something with your mind. What I did, was as the radiation rays passed through me, I sent the rays to a whole list of people who needed help and healing.

"Think of Herald as an entity that comes to heal you. As the transforming elements of radiation and chemo go into you, they will help transform Herald into a mist, a vapor that will go out like compassion to nourish the countryside."

Deborah closes this incredible conversation with these words "Here's Herald, bless his heart, such a gift, transforming into healing energy to send out to others…."

Then she promised to send me a book in which she wrote a chapter. The book is called *The Pagan Book of Living and Dying* by Starhawk. It arrived a few days later and proved to be an invaluable source of both spiritual counsel and practical tools and techniques to deal with the dying process for others or oneself.

After we hung up I walked on a cloud for the rest of the day. It's like my head was turned around and my perspective with it, a necessary turning! I began Drawing 5, an image of Herald in various stages of change from tumor/killer/rage into compassionate cool waters and mist going out to nourish creation. At last I have my image and I deeply feel it is a win-win one for both Herald and me.

Drawing 5 went fast, it just flowed out. The power of the image of Herald transmuting from a base form into a higher evolutionary form while Magenta, my guardian angel, looked on in blessing sustained me for many weeks.

My daughter Sarah comes for a visit from her home in Oklahoma City. I share all these things with her. She has the capacity to understand and support my process and I am very grateful. My step daughter, Amy, who lives fairly close, came for dinner with us one evening and we had a good laugh over the drawings, especially the "Save A Rectum" angel parade with Herald leading.

INITIATION DAY 19, A DIFFICULT TIME

I wrote in my journal: My initiation is a bit heavy on me yesterday and today. All the indignities, the poking, the invasion of my private parts. Cold instruments in my vagina and my anus. Strangers walking about while I am laid out on a hard board for one hour and fifteen minutes, nude from the waist down, uncomfortable, embarrassed, ankles taped to the table so I don't move.

It is an important time as the radiation oncologist, Dr. Kiel, and members of her team, are using laser technology and positioning the radiation entry points for the therapy that is to begin in a few days. It's a time for great skill and expertise. Precision is essential. What they decide today will last for the entire treatment.

There's trouble with the complex, sensitive and temperamental equipment delaying things. Finally I get tattoos on my fanny for the three entry points and it hurts. No wonder I've never gotten a tattoo! But tattoo's last and won't wash off in the shower and tub.

If I'd known then what I know now, I would have asked for a blanket to cover the parts of me that were not essential to the procedure, but I was too overwhelmed with the system that I had been catapulted into, too much a novice. So I endured in silence, trying to be a 'good sport.' But when I got home I cried at the indignity of it all.

The day before was also full of examinations, people's fingers in my private parts, bodily functions discussed at great length. I'm weighed, measured and examined over and over again by each doctor on the team in their separate offices. And oh my, I guess I need to complain a bit. I'm weary of my life taken over by this great interruption.

A MESSAGE FROM STAR-THROWER

Dear One,

Sure, you must complain, that's part of your authentic experience. In a way it's funny, its part of the ridiculousness, the impossibility, the absurdity, the indignity of having a body.

Laugh, cry, rail, praise—the whole range is yours to enjoy.

Did you like my friend Deborah? Did you notice how easily the connection was made and how rich it was?

May 4/00
Initiation Day 20
Herald's lava form is transmuted to healing mist that goes forth and nourishes
5.

INITIATION DAY 21, AT THE FARM

How can I sing the praises of the farm enough? It is such a soul home for me. I don't think I've told you anything about my little farm yet. Well, I bought a small part of a larger ecological and conservation project called Tryon Farm near Michigan City, Indiana.

An architect, Ed Noonan, who I swear is also a zen master of some sort, bought a 165-acre farm about an hour drive from my Chicago apartment. Concerned by the thoughtless urban sprawl going on like a giant cancer all over our country, Ed decided to design a new way for people to live together. He wants them to have a sense of space and country living while still honoring the fact that nature and plants and creatures also need space. He came up with a win-win situation—there's that phrase again! Working with the Departments of Natural Resources and Fish and Wildlife, the natural wetlands here are being restored, meadows cleansed of exotic or nonindigenous plants and renewed, clogged stream beds cleared, forests honored. The latest plan is to bring in a herd of cows to eat the forest undergrowth as it is too thick.

Ed's plan is to build about 5 "settlements" of simple, inexpensive, small homes. Each settlement will be built using the latest in ecologically sound building materials. About 60 acres will be built and the rest will remain natural and shared. There are no lawns, no street lights, no driveways. Garages are clustered and people walk to their homes along gravel paths through the natural landscape. I bought a little red wagon to haul groceries and other items. There is no artificial lighting outdoors, so, if its dark and the moon isn't out, bring a good flashlight!

The greatness of Ed's plan is that we can see the stars at night, enjoy the music of nature as we tune into her beautiful, subtle sounds. We have meadows, forests, streams and wetlands as our landscaping. From our windows, porches and decks we can watch the show nature puts on every day without interrupting it too much. The people here are so much fun and I love the three goats, the chickens and the organic vegetable garden.

I feel as though I am living closer to nature than ever before. The wildlife brings constant echoes of something wild in my heart that needs space to grow and be. All night long the chorus frogs sing and sing in the spring wetlands.

I moved into my farmhouse Thanksgiving last year. Now it's May 5th and I love planning and planting my little courtyard garden, it nourishes me. The city provides a different life, a good life, but no garden for those who live in a high-rise building! Each unit here has what Ed calls an outdoor room, complete with a few framed openings, like windows, to widen the view. In this space we can do whatever we want and the deer or other creatures can't get in and eat it all up.

My life is so full and rich with blessings and this moment, this very moment, couldn't be better. Suddenly, my artistic block disappearing, I complete the drawing I label Drawing 6.

"Forgiveness is to offer
no resistance to life . . .
to let life flow
through you."
Eckhardt Tolle
PAST
NOW
NOW
NOW
NOW
FUTURE
May 5, '00

COLORECTAL TREATMENT PROGRAM

The colorectal surgeon, Dr. Stryker, at Northwestern University Hospital has given me a time-line for my process of treatment. First, some preparation for an intensive five-and-a-half-week chemotherapy and radiation program. This includes a surgical procedure putting a 'port' in my shoulder just below the collar bone accessing a major vein near my heart. This 'port' will be used for a drip system allowing smaller doses of chemo to go in my body 24 hours a day. Radiation would be daily except weekends. Giving chemo and radiation before surgery is a fairly new strategy. Dr. Stryker mentioned in passing that in 10-15% of the cases the chemo and radiation is enough to cause the tumor to completely disappear.

After all that plus four weeks of healing from the side effects, there would be further tests to see what was accomplished. Then surgery to remove any remaining diseased tissue while checking my lymph nodes and other sites for signs of cancer.

A colostomy for a couple months would leave my bowel free to heal. Then more surgery to remove the colostomy, reconnecting the bowel. Finally a procedure to remove the port. I figure all these interventions would take about six months to complete and chances are good that I would be healed by Thanksgiving.

I CLAIM A DIFFERENT PATH

After returning home I begin to think of all the doctor has said, especially the part about the tumor disappearing for some patients. I decide that I want to be one of the 10-15% for whom that happens! I begin to ask all my allies to pray for, to hold in their minds, to hold the intention—whatever their way is—that this be true for me.

My voice begins getting stronger. At first I notice I ask for this in a small voice, full of doubt. Then my voice becomes bolder, stronger, and finally with vigor I assert that I want to be part of the 10-15%! I move from I don't deserve to ask this for myself to knowing I have every right to hold this intention!

CHAPTER THREE

THE ANTIDOTE IS IN THE VENOM

What we thought
would be a boundary
that we wouldn't trespass
becomes
the horizon for an exciting journey
into
worlds uncharted.

Manuela Mascetti

INITIATION DAY 22, THE ROOT OF IT ALL

I used to state that I'd never have chemo and/or radiation. If cancer came, I'd just die, "…a boundary that I wouldn't trespass." However, I am not ambivalent about taking them now. I feel strongly that this is the right path for me at this time. I am surprised at how much I am embracing life these days and how willing I am to pay a high price to achieve it!

Part of the price is having to lay aside the life I had planned to live this life that is coming to me. I canceled two trips I had really looked forward to. I dropped out of classes I'd planned to take. I canceled board meetings, speaking engagements, updating my web site. I turned down social engagements, wedding invitations and family reunions.

Instead I found myself cleaning my apartment, getting some new pj's and housecoats. Catching up on my desk work. Getting my hair cut short. I am preparing myself, simplifying my life, making sure my will is in order, checking my power of attorney for health care. My daughter, Sarah, offered to take my cats and I am not to worry. I find a home with my nephew, Brad and family for my fish friends. It seems important to tie up the loose ends of my life.

Remember those guides that came to me in December of 1999, those books that 'jumped' off the shelves into my arms? Well, one of them becomes again, a vital guide. It is another poem by Rumi, the poem cards 'just happened' to have this one on top this morning:

> Don't go away, come near.
> Don't be faithless, be faithful.
> Find the antidote in the venom.
> Come to the root of the root of yourself.

Well, here is a teaching for me! In my cancer itself, is the antidote. Herald has the answer for my healing. This poem confirms all of the insights that have been coming to me.

And the root of myself—well, the tumor was certainly at the root of my body, the base of my spine, the end of my digestive system, the root 'chakra' to use the language of that ancient thought system. Again, I am asked to look at where Herald is and listen to what that might mean. In the book of interpretations and explanations that goes along with the poems, author Manuela Mascetti begins the explanation of Rumi's little poem by writing: "What's so scary about intimacy?"

A LAUGH AT STAR-THROWER'S SENSE OF HUMOR!

At this point I begin to laugh! I think dear Star-Thrower, you are a curve-thrower too! What's so scary about intimacy? What's so scary about intimacy! I can't believe I just read that out of all the possible things I could have read today!

I spent last night thinking of the suffering that goes on in families, scarring the coming generations. Thinking of the suffering that went on in my family, my mother's family, my father's family and the families of their parents and grandparents. There was no safety in these families for women and children. What's so scary about intimacy? That's what's scary! Mascetti goes on to write:

> The fear is that in the surrender to love we will surrender to the will of the other and become a slave. We need to make an important distinction: When we open our heart, we surrender to love, not to the other. Love is our own, it is a quality of our heart, it is akin to courage. It is also the only power that can bring true and long-lasting transformation. When we love, we don't disempower ourselves; on the contrary, our heart is full and our vision clear.

She concludes her comments on this Rumi poem by saying "Conquering fear, coming near—this is being at the root of the root of yourself. <u>This is the place where we love most and best.</u>" The underlining is mine. I feel this is a key sentence for me and part of the urgent message both the

Rumi poem and Herald bring. At the root of the root of my deepest self lies the key to my ability to love well.

CONQUERING FEAR, COMING NEAR

I have not known how to love very well. There have been so many relationship disappointments in spite of what I perceived to be my best efforts. These disappointments motivated me to be on a journey to unravel some of the confusions of my life, to figure out who I am and what is really happening.

A deep fear is surfacing. I realize I have the sabotaging belief that if I am intimate with a man in a family situation my life will be in danger, not only mine but my children's as well. If I am real, stop playing any games, stop fitting into other's images of what they want me to be, I won't get my needs met and furthermore, my life will be at risk.

When I look at this belief, I can see it is so illogical! In fact it's a big lie! There's no way my life is in jeopardy or ever has been! Yet this is a belief I have operated from on a deeply unconscious level.

A big piece of my story is just now going into place. I want to tell you that story briefly because it has everything to do with my cancer, with Herald's message to me and with the Rumi poem about the root of the root of myself.

FAMILY LEGACIES

It was November, 1921, darkness had already fallen when my grandfather on my mother's side tried to murder his wife and his 6 daughters. His only son had been killed by a speeding train just weeks before and something snapped. He attacked his wife first, smashing her head with a lead pipe and leaving her for dead on the living room floor. He then began on the girls. My mother was 13 at the time, he dragged her out from under the bed where she was hiding and hit her on the head. This went on through two more daughters before one of the older girls got help and he was stopped. He spent the rest of his life in a prison for the criminally insane.

It took months of hospitalization before the girls and their mother were ready to go home and try to put the pieces of their lives back together. Three of the girls carried scars on their foreheads for life. My grandmother had a depression in her forehead that went deep, her eyes could not work together, she lost her sense of smell. Grandma wore a wig that came down below her eyebrows to hide the disfigurement. Sitting on her lap as a little child, I used to lift up her wig and ask her what happened "Oh I was in an automobile accident."

There was so much shame connected with this incident that it became one of those family secrets. I didn't find out until I was over 40. My aunts, mother's sisters, told me so I could better understand what happened to mother and why she handled life as she did.

Mother married a man with the same violence and deprivation in his make-up. He came from a line of impulsive, rageaholics who used religion to dominate. My father blamed and hated his mother for abandoning him and he punished my mother for his wound with his cruelty, tantrums and moods.

As a little girl, I watched father hurting her over and over. I saw that she was incapable of doing anything to protect us or change the pattern. She had a survivor mentality, she just tried harder to please and manipulate him. We walked on tiptoe around the house so as not to do anything to set father off. Over the years I could see what he was slowly killing her. He lived 25 years longer than she. I hated him, feared him and vowed never to marry a man like him. Yet, he had a much more interesting life as a pioneer aviator than mother did as a housewife! I wished I was a boy. I saw little about the role of women that appealed to me.

PRISONERS TO OUR BELIEFS

Because the pattern of violence against women and children had gone on for a number of generations in my family lineage, fear of men came to me with my mother's milk. It was buried deep in my unconscious and I lived most of my life not knowing it existed in spite of years of therapy.

Dark fear seemed to taint my actions and reactions to men, leaving me feeling vulnerable and confused. I have been in three marriages, two ended in divorce, one after 16 years, one after 7. My last marriage ended after 13 years with my husband's long terminal illness.

Gradually I have taken increasing responsibility for my confusion. I've come to see my part in 'co-creating' all the drama and suffering. I finally realize that my unhappiness was not caused by others, they only brought out the pain and unhappiness that was already in me.

So, I am moving from feeling like a confused victim. How? By staying with my difficult feelings and confusions, by seeking wise counsel, by not giving up until my wound is uncovered, the wound which was triggered by the behavior of the men in my life.

LETTING MY SON'S CHOICES PUT MY LIFE AT RISK

Without appropriate knowledge and consciousness, we repeat our ancestral patterns over and over again. My life shows this so clearly. The most recent example of allowing myself to be depleted until my life became jeopardized was with my grown son. I love him deeply and has been hard for me to let him go into the drug world he has chosen. I didn't until my health was at risk and I realized that I could do no more.

Last March, I went to see him on the west coast to help celebrate his 39th birthday. I stayed with an old friend, Bobbie Hanson, since he was in the process of moving from his apartment. He was lonely and depressed because his wife had left (she was right in doing so) and his business was failing.

Until I saw him I didn't know how far gone he was. But when I saw how bizarre his behavior had gotten, the abusive way he treated people including me, how poor his judgment and how awful he looked, I had to face the truth. He refused all treatment saying "I've done all that a couple times, I know exactly what they'll say and I don't need to hear it again. I'm OK, I can handle this myself."

I could no longer fool myself and live on the hope that his beautiful side would come back and that we would enjoy each other again. March 14, his birthday, came and I knew I couldn't be with him. I wrote a letter and left it where he would find it. In the letter I said many things ending with:

> ... all I care about is that your thirst for freedom is quenched and your hunger for healthy, loyal companionship met. Right now, I have to love you from a distance because when I am around you I find myself slipping into depression. My nights are difficult as I toss and turn with worry over you. My digestive track is bleeding, my health at risk with the stress.
>
> I could not love you if I did not care well for myself. Your behaviors at the present are toxic for me and so I am taking a break from you. Let's check in with each other in a month...April 14. Meanwhile each day you are in my heart and prayers.

April 14 was the day I found out I had cancer.

MY DEEPEST ROOT'S GIFTS

Until we know ourselves down to our deepest root or 'core issue' as my therapist friends say, we keep ourselves bound, unable to love as freely and courageously as we want to. So facing our deepest fears, finding the antidote in the venom and exploring the things that frighten us the most, can lead to our being better people, better· lovers.

If the truth of my cancer lies in Herald and his killer rage and the antidote is there as well, what is this truth that will heal me? To recognize the deep belief system that came to me through my family line "If you are close to a man, your life and your children's lives will be jeopardized." To find ways to dismantle that belief and thereby break the pattern binding me from my true potential.

To enjoy the gifts that will flood into the space made available, like the ability to "find the place where we love most and best." This is when I did Drawing 7.

Dear One, Welcome to the root of the root of yourself! Welcome to your deepest heart that lives there!

I'm so glad you got my joke about what's so scary about intimacy! I'm glad you got the message and connected it all together. My message is one of liberation and power—for you, yes, but also for others. This is a profound issue on earth. In so many marriages, the people are killing each other. The relationships between women and men reflect the deep crisis in which humanity now finds itself.

You are doing so well. You are mining the treasures Herald is bringing. There is more goodness to come, so stay alert!

Love, Star-Thrower

INITIATION DAY 27, MAY 11, FATHER'S BIRTHDAY

Today is the anniversary of my father's birthday. I wake up with a shocking dream. Maybe he is giving me a gift from his transformed state on the other side. The dream is certainly full of promise:

A group of us are together at an old farm type house in the country. It is time to head home. We can't find our own car, so we borrow an old, rusty, beat-up, white van and get in. My son is in the front seat by me, the others climb in back, I am the driver.

The driveway is a dirt two lane affair. We are parked by the house on a slight hill that leads down into a small pond.

I get out of the van to return to the house to get something. I look out the window and see the van slowly rolling down the hill. It halts then rolls again then halts. It rolls into the pond. Everyone gets out. I learned later that my son made attempts to stop the van but they failed.

Then I realize the pond is really a cesspool, thick with gunk and junk like old refrigerators, etc.

I begin to arrange for AAA to come and pull the van out when suddenly there is a loud noise and a large explosion. The van goes up into a thousand blazing pieces. How good that no one was in it, maybe we were all saved from being killed by being out of it!

"Don't go away,
come near,
Don't be faithless,
be faithful.
Find the antidote
in the venum.
Come to the root
of the root
of yourself."
Rumi

May 6, 00
Initiation Day 22
7.

MEANINGS AND INTERPRETATIONS

Obviously this is a powerful dream saying that something has exploded, been dismantled. I give you some of my thoughts on what some of the symbols mean to me.

Van Symbol:
A borrowed conveyance, old, rusty, beat-up. A van helps a group get around (like a belief system does). White, identified with being right, good, godly, like my father's line, Methodists, hell believing, Bible quoting, domineering men.

I see the van as having a mind of its own without concern for others. Just like a family pattern that is unconscious and cares not who gets hurt. The van will not be stopped on its roll but goes into the cesspool of junk and explodes, never to be put together again. If the people had stayed in the van, they would have exploded too!

Old Farm House Symbol:
My lineage on the male side, grandfather and great grandfather were all farmers.

Pond Symbol:
What appears to be one thing is another. What I thought was a nice little pond in the countryside is a cesspool of junk, but I was not conscious of that at first.

I Am The Driver Symbol:
I used to have dreams where I wasn't driving. I'd given my power away, so this dream shows progress! However, I am in a borrowed conveyance, my own misplaced somewhere. That's what happens when we are living out a pattern that is not our own. We are not living our own destiny.

DREAM PROMISE

This dream is full of promise that the ancestral pattern I had been caught in has exploded, is transformed. The dream looks violent, but in truth it represents the spiritual fire or life force required to dismantle and restructure old patterns within our personality so that which is actual and true within our nature can be expressed and restored.

The dream promises that family and cultural conditioning have loosened their grip and I am free to see more clearly who I am and what I want. This information will come to me through various synchronicities, insights, wake-up calls and peak experiences.

My life is full of miracles these days, full of peak experiences and synchronicities. Cancer itself is a big wake-up call. Herald's message has become clear and I thank his little self! Drawing 8 tells part of the dream story.

Dream, May 11,
Initiation Day #27

—ஒ❖ல—

CHAPTER FOUR

SIDE EFFECTS

Whatever the present moment contains,
accept it as if you had chosen it.
Always work with it.
Make it your friend and ally,
not your enemy.
This will miraculously transform
your whole life.

Eckhart Tolle

INITIATION DAY 28, THE THERAPIES BEGIN

Such a full day yesterday at Northwestern Hospital! Dr. Hartz put in the port. I had my first radiation treatment. Chemo is dripping into my vena cava (I think that is what the vein's name is). Some good news; there are different kinds of chemo. The side effects of the type I'm to receive do not usually include losing one's hair.

Naomi, my sister-in-law, felt I needed someone to be with me for the first radiation treatment. As a nurse, she could explain what was happening to me. The radiation team let her look at all the hi-tech instruments. It is all a bit awesome for someone like me who knows so little about the medical side of life.

Jackie, Marianne and Patti all join me in the afternoon while I wait for the port implanting surgery. We laugh, joke and pass the time. They were waiting for me when I came out of surgery. They helped me dress and made sure I got to my next procedure which was to install the chemo system.

Initiation Day 28
May 12, 2000
Rituals of Arousal in the "Temple of Healing"
9.

I have such a sense of anticipation for my process of therapy. It is hard to describe but I know that whatever the venom of this cancer, there is a gift inside of such magnitude that I hardly know how to speak of it.

Drawing 9 flowed from my pens. Check out the musical blue mist coming from where Herald is positioned. He is transmuting already! Also, note that Magenta has fingers now—sort of. I'm learning!

A CONVERSATION WITH STAR-THROWER

Dear Star-Thrower, I don't know what is happening inside me, but I feel so supported, I do not feel lonely and sort of 'at sea' in my life anymore. Instead I feel full, on target, on my path. I feel loved and supported as kindness' shower upon me from every direction.

What is the dynamic here? Is it the care, empathy and affirmation I am receiving because I have cancer? Is it having a purpose in life so clearly before me—the transmutation of Herald? Do I feel easier with people because I have something up front to talk about, the big "C"? Because I can talk of my cancer and am living out most people's worst fear, I get attention and that makes me feel good? And, by having a 'good' experience, seeming to be brave and all that I get positive strokes, does this make me feel good? I don't know. All I know is that I am happy, I feel good, and this process is so filled with blessings that I watch it all with gratitude, wonder and humor.

I think I'll just put all these thoughts aside, they can go on forever and ever and really go nowhere. I'll just say a big thank you to life, to my guardian angel, Magenta, to you, Star Thrower and to the Temple of Healing with all its ministers and priests. Thank you for such a temple only blocks from where I live. The convenience of everything blows my mind! I feel I'm on a fast train to somewhere glorious with people who are glorious too.

I receive a response from Star-Thrower. In fact it turns into a conversation.

Dear One, everything will be Just fine, now and always—now and always. Rest in this. Count on this. Allis well.

Let's speak of your will to Jive, can you feel the strength of your life force these days? It's stronger than its been for years—how do you account for this?

Well, Great Friend, is it because I've found our connection and finally know I am valued and loved? I'm accompanied on this journey by a Great Friend so I'm not so alone? These are all such powerful dynamics in my life for which I am sooooo grateful!

Dear one, yes, you are, and your gratitude opens the way for ever more gifts of Jove from Love. Magenta sends her blessings, she enjoys being featured in your art!

INITIATION DAY 31, AFTER MOTHER'S DAY

I didn't know how much that day, Mother's Day, would sting. My son was one who said nice things, sent flowers, and was thoughtful. I miss that tender part of him. I miss him. So the tears are close to the surface.

The chemo pack is a very real presence in my life. I'm tethered to it night and day. It goes into the bath with me and waits on the side of the tub. It lays beside me on the bed all night. It only weighs a few pounds, but by the end of the day, it begins to feel heavy.

Yesterday, a young woman friend noticed the chemo pack I wear with the tubes connecting things. She asked: "What does it feel like, having poison going into your veins all the time?" I assured her that I don't see it that way. Then I sang her a little ditty I made up to the tune of London Bridge.

> Rainbow healing is flowing in,
> flowing in,
> flowing in,
>
> Rainbow healing is flowing in,
> My fair lady!

I sing this to myself whenever I think of the chemo process. See Drawing 10 for my image of how the chemo was helping to heal Herald and me. I'm beginning to draw lines in my face so I don't look too young.

INITIATION DAY 34, EIGHTH DAY OF CHEMO AND RADIATION

I am surprised at myself, I astonish myself with my good spirits and my non-resistance or acceptance of life as it is coming to me. Yes, I astonish myself.

My friend Patty Woerner sent me a new book of poetry by Hafiz, the 14th Century Persian poet that I have fallen in love with. I am touched by her thoughtfulness and greedily begin to absorb some of the poetry. It is a time of spiritual highs for me.

Rainbow healing is
flowing in,
flowing in,
flowing in,
Rainbow healing is
flowing in
My fair lady!

Rainbow light is
healing Herald
healing Herald
healing Herald
Rainbow light is
healing Herald
My fair lady!

May 15, '00
Initiation Day 31

Rituals of the Temple of Healing

10.

Come drink from the Heart of the Friend.
Come let your every cell and the eye of your soul know
the Resplendent Nourishment and Compassion,
the Divine Beauty and Grace
of the ever present
Ancient one.

Drawing 11 grew out of this poetry. That's what is happening to me, I am being nourished drinking celestial water from the heart of the Friend!

These poems influence me profoundly I am in tears one minute then laughing another. Drawing 12 comes from the first half of a poem titled *In a Tree House* and I write part of the poem on the drawing.

"Love will surely bust you wide open into an unfettered, blooming, new galaxy." Those words grab me as this is exactly what's happening to me. I am being *bust* wide open as another fetter is being transmuted through Herald.

I repeat these words over and over during my days. Soaking them in. I have so longed for this—my core longing—to be loved by and in love with Star-Thrower, the Great Friend.

INITIATION DAY 37, FEARS CREEP IN

I am feeling a bit blah. Nothing is going right. I shop for porch furniture for my farm house since the May weather is so pleasant, only I can't find anything I like. Besides my energy runs out.

My body does not feel good. I must stay pretty close to a bathroom. I have trouble with all the disciplines, the pill-taking and juicing the green leaves. My stomach feels queasy.

I finish reading the well written autobiographical book REFUGE by Terry Tempest Williams about her mother's cancer and death. It depresses me. The suffering and struggles of the whole family sink into me far deeper than I want.

Williams has such a heart for nature and describes some of the traumas nature is enduring in her home state of Utah as a result of human greed and ignorance. This too depresses me. I realize I must choose carefully what I read during this time, as I am especially sensitive. I don't watch the news right now, nor do I read the paper. I can't take on the sufferings and horrors of the world.

May 18, '00
Day 34 of my
Initiation

Light will someday
split you wide open...
for a divine seed,
the crown of destiny,
is hidden and sown
on an ancient,
fertile plain.
You hold the
title to.
Love will surely
burst you wide open
into an unfettered, blooming new
galaxy.....
Hafiz
May 20, 06
Initiation Day 36
12.

I keep remembering the message from Star-Thrower "It is not your time to die, and it will not be hard." I keep thinking that my body created Herald, the killer. What a mystery. I wonder if all my art and my 'take' on my process are just bogus. There, I have said it. What if all this is just bogus.

I will try listening and see if Star-Thrower can give me a helpful message. I can't hear anything. I feel afraid. I feel out of touch. I long for connection with the Friend.

Yes, that connection is everything isn't it. I am deep inside you. I am in Herald, I am in the root of your root, I am in you, you are in me.

Do not become Jost in the unhappy experience of Terry and her mother. You know not their full story. Stay close to yourself and to your experience. You know what you know now trust that. You know what you know!

Cancer is such a scary concept on your planet. The fear is the real killer. Your fear level is way down and your acceptance level is way up—you stay with that and feel me dancing with you and Herald. Dancing away the tumor and the patterns it represents. Dancing until you are so happy and free you will bring my truth of happiness and freedom to many others.

Blessings this day. I have some gifts for you. Watch!

INITIATION DAY 38, I'M ON MY WAY DOWN

It's Monday and I arrive back in Chicago from the farm ready for the new week. I am concerned because my face has developed burn marks all over it. My tongue is so sensitive I don't want my ritual hot tea and milk in the mornings—now that is a big deal! The ulcers in my mouth are hurting beyond my ability to be a good sport and my bottom lip, oh how my swollen bottom lip throbs. My feet burn and I hobble about in soft bedroom slippers when possible. My fanny burns and my bowels are under siege.

I begin to worry because it isn't even 2 weeks of treatment yet and I have 5 1/2 week's total. I have to admit that I find things hard when I wonder how hard it might get....

INITIATION DAY 39, I HIT BOTTOM

I reach my limit. Interesting that I dress for the day in black. I have an appointment with my lawyer at Sidley and Austin so I want to look conservative. My mouth is so sore that if something funny happens I have to hold my mouth closed so as not to crack my lips with a smile.

I wish I could check in with a doctor but Dr. Tellez, the chemo doctor, is on vacation. Dr. Kiel with radiation has just returned from vacation and I do not have an appointment with her for two more days. I am beginning to feel like a victim as I have not seen a doctor since before chemo and radiation began. Not enjoying that victim feeling, I call the chemo department and the nurse Heidi takes me seriously. "Come right in and see Dr. Merrill who is covering for Dr. Tellez."

I stop at the grocery on my way. Something terrible is happening to my personality. I am ever so irritable and judgmental! I am critical of the grocery check-out girl's lipstick color. I am angry because the stop light turns red. And who are all those dumb people crowding Michigan Ave and crossing the street just when I need to make a turn in my car? I find myself judging every race and ethnic group including mine for our irritating aspects! With Chicago so blessed with a usually much enjoyed diversity the opportunities for judging are plentiful!

In a snit, I arrive at the doctor's offices. I am weighed (that always puts me in a bad mood, except that I am losing weight and that helps), given a blood test and put in a room to wait. The minutes tick by. I brought a book but I don't want to read it.

Actually I am hardly interested in anything but myself these days. I can't even lose myself in a book by a favorite author such as Elizabeth Peters and her Egyptian intrigue novels. They usually delight me. I've had this book of hers for over a month. It goes to all my doctors' appointments, sits on my night stand, gets carried back and forth between the farm and Chicago. The book looks as though 50 people had read it and I'm only half through.

I am kept waiting until I begin to pace the halls. No one notices me. Everyone is busy, phones ringing and ringing. I find a much needed bathroom then pace again. My radiation appointment is coming up and my time is limited. Feeling abandoned by everyone including the Great Friend I write on a piece of paper: Three 3 things I want right now! 1) I want to feel Star Thrower's presence, 2) I want relief from chemo for a few days and 3) I want Dr. Merrill to come into my examining room soon.

I go back out into the halls and pace.

About then a nice looking gray haired doctor says "Are you Ms Hardin?" (Inside the medical community my Dr. title is not recognized. Today it irritates me! I feel so disempowered on other levels, I at least want to be recognized as a doctor in my field!) I say yes. "I've been looking for you, what can I do for you?" I hand him my list of complaints. He reads them over and looks in my mouth. "We've got to get you off chemo. This is unusual. You are very sensitive, nothing wrong with that. Taking you off chemo won't hurt your process."

He goes into the chemo station and announces to the nurses: "Take her off chemo immediately." Within a few minutes I am free of the fanny pack, the whirring motor, the tubes and bandages. Whew! I realize that I want to cry. I had been listened to, my complaints were not minimized, I was taken seriously and my needs acted on immediately.

ANOTHER RECOGNITION

My life-shaping experience as a child came back forcefully. I was not listened to. I felt guilty when I expressed wants or needs. In truth, mother and father had all the needs and I was not to disturb them.

Maybe this Initiation will bring a further healing. I will recognize more quickly my right to have needs and then I will act on them. I will also complain as necessary to an appropriate person and make sure I am heard. I will not be stoic. I will not wait until I am about to scream and I will not be a victim.

On my way home as I drive my car down the levels of the gigantic hospital parking lot, I pass a car with the license plate 'CA DREAM.' I take this for a communication from Star Thrower and so I journal:

> My Dream: To Transmute along with Herald into a higher form from a baser form.
>
> To Be in the Flow, not making things hard. I want to be peacefully, organically and easily carried along by Star Power.
>
> To Complete this Initiation by the end of June. I want healthy tissue at my root chakra. I want Herald transmuted into compassion, no surgery, no colostomy, only health.
>
> To Write a Book of this process that could bless others in their Initiations whatever they be.

Arriving home I eat applesauce for dinner and go to bed. I am in bed very early these days. It is a difficult night as the burning and throbbing of my lip, the ulcers in my mouth, my burning feet, plus the cramping and rumbling of my bowels keep me sleepless.

INITIATION DAY 40, A DAY TO CRY

This seems to be my day to cry. I cry first thing in the morning as I look in the mirror at my swollen red nose, my sore lip, the nasty, red burns on my right cheek. I cry hobbling in my slippers about my apartment. I cry when loving friends call to see how I am. In my meditation time I begin Drawing 13, not sure how to express what I am feeling.

I decide to cancel my radiation too, just take a break, go to the farm early and heal over the Memorial Day holiday. I will take charge of my process! Yes, that is the way to deal with this! Wow, to have some time to shop for my screened porch, to have some free time not used by hospitals and therapies. I begin to feel empowered.

In reality, how skewed my priorities had become! I want to quit the painful yet necessary treatment and shop for my porch.

I call radiation and ask to speak to Dr. Kiel, to check with her about all this. However no return call from the busy doctor. So, taking charge of my life, I call radiation to cancel my 3:30 appointment. The nurse hands me over to the radiologist, Paul, Paul hands me over to Dr. Keil (he was able to find her). Dr. Keil warns me that this would be injurious to my health. "Radiation is different from chemo, it needs consistency. Besides, it is too early to have much reaction to the radiation yet. You must continue."

I am so disappointed I cry—just what I didn't want to do! Between sniffles I read her my long list of complaints. To each one she says "That's the chemo, that's the chemo. Come in and see me before your radiation appointment this afternoon, I can give you some things that will help."

Too soon I am back at the hospital. Dr. Keil is busy. Finally I see Toi, an aid, who comes to take me back to radiation for my treatment. She asks me how I am and I respond "Crying, today is my day to cry." "Ohhhh," she croons, "I'm so sorry, its important to cry sometimes!" and with that she puts her arms around me in a big warm hug—right in the sterile white hall of the radiation department.

The hug gives me the courage to tell her I am supposed to see Dr. Keil before treatment (why does it take so much push and courage to keep taking charge of my own process and standing up for my rights?). Dr. Keil magically appears and we go into an examining room.

Within a few minutes, I have my hands full of resources: ointments, soothing suppositories, pills, prescriptions, sympathy and encouragement. Of course I am crying most of the time, my sunglasses on.

In radiation I take my sunglasses off in order to lie down on that hard plank, fanny bared. The radiologists all commiserate with me and allow as how they have some crying days too. No one shames me or makes me feel foolish.

Once that big radiation machine whirrs into place and I am alone in the room, I begin to cry harder, nose dripping into the space under my face. When the ray is turned on with its strong hummm, sorrow like a tidal wave wants to pull me into another realm. But I can't go there because I am afraid my sobs will take over and I'll shake and the ray will hit the wrong place.

Exhausted, I return home for a brief rest before my friend, Marianne, drives me to Dr. Howard's Wellness Associates. I have an acupuncture treatment with Master Wong. Marianne wants to be with me as she knows things are difficult right now. She chides me for not telling her earlier how hard it was.

I feel better after the acupuncture treatment and a good talk with Dr. Howard. I even take my sunglasses off.

Marianne lives on the floor just below me in our apartment building. She brings her dinner upstairs to eat with me. I could not eat and so I lie on the couch. We talk. Marianne rubs my feet and succeeds in bringing down their temperature some. I work more on Drawing 13. I want it to express something of how cut off I feel from Magenta and the Friend. The toughest part is not being able to feel the Friend nearby.

Come, join the courageous
who have no choice.
But to let their entire world
that endure,

Indeed, God is Real.
— Hafiz
The Gift 24 / Invitation slash 40

13.

NOW, THE BIG QUESTION

In view of these difficulties I face the question: Did I not hear the Star Thrower rightly? Am I deluding myself when I thought I heard in my heart that not only would I live but that this process would not be hard? My fear is that I didn't really hear those things, and that Star Thrower is just a piece of imagination with no reality behind it.

Then the poet Hafiz gives me the words I need:

> Come join the courageous
> Who have no choice
> But to bet their entire world
> That indeed,
> Indeed, God is real.

That is what I am doing and must continue to do. Bet my entire world that the Friend exists and that what I am experiencing is a real relationship. Not just a mirage. Not a fantasy born of need.

CHAPTER FIVE

PAIN MANAGEMENT

Just sit there right now.
Don't do a thing.
Just rest.

For your separation from God
Is the hardest work in this world.

Let me bring you trays of food
And something
That you like to drink.

You can use my soft words
As a cushion
For your
Head.

Hafiz

INITIATION DAY 45, I GET SOME ANSWERS

Last week had some difficult moments. Perhaps the most difficult part was wondering if I only imagined Star-Thrower's promise to me "You will live and it will not be hard."

Dear Star-Seer, I know your questions. I know your pain. It was a week of ups and downs. Everything that happened is useful and integral to whom you are becoming. Nothing, nothing is for nothing.

What you are enduring is part of the human experience. What you are experiencing is something everyone can identify with, it is a vehicle through which your courage and your beautiful spirit can shine.

Star-Thrower, this morning's gift poem from Rumi was on promises. How apt!

> There are true promises
> that make the heart grateful
> there are false promises
> fraught with disquiet.
> The promise of the noble is sterling;
> the promise of the unworthy
> breeds anguish of the soul.

The most powerful part of this poem card was the picture on the back, an ancient Persian art work with a mystical message. There is a bucolic scene of trees and hills with a rushing stream cascading down the hillside. Crossing the stream on foot, with long strides, is a strong individual carrying on his shoulders a black horse and its rider.

What an image! I wonder what the ancient artist had experienced in order to even come up with such a powerful and unusual image. In view of my situation, I take in the message that: 1) There is a rough crossing to be crossed; 2) The Great Strong Friend is carrying me; 3) Not only me but my horse power (stretches my mind, that part!) and 4) The three of us are not quite half way across.

This image supports me as I recover from the chemo side effects and continue with radiation. I begin feeling better and better. My mouth heals in three days, my feet even sooner. Even the burn marks on my face fade leaving only the faintest scars. I begin finding my days to be as jewels again, from beginning to end.

I learn important lessons from last week: 1) Use temporary or "seeming" setbacks as a timet to affirm that I am on the path; 2) Star-Thrower is real; 3) Star-Thrower's promises are noble and true; 4) I am being carried like the person and the horse across the fast flowing stream—not as in helpless, but as in support for those times of great difficulty and challenge.

INITIATION DAY 48, AN UNUSUAL MESSENGER

It is early in the morning on this beautiful June 1. Today is the day when I begin chemotherapy again, only this time at half the dose intensity. I sit in my city living room feeling so good and watching the sun rise over Lake Michigan. In my journal I write to Star Thrower "I don't have anything to say. I sit here feeling life around me, feeling you with me and that is enough."

Just at that moment, one of my cats, Bastet (named for the Egyptian cat goddess), who was sound asleep and had been for some time hops from her cozy spot and comes to me. She begins her ritual to get my attention, patting and pawing at my leg.

"Hello Bastet, what do you want? My lap is full with my journal…."

Paw, paw, is her response.

So I put my journal aside and make a lap space for her. She lightly jumps up and stands there looking at me, unblinking, her green eyes seeking mine. She waits for me to free my hand from holding my pen and caress her.

"Bastet, you are such a lesson to me about how to be with Star Thrower and my friends. I must, without feeling like a bother, jump on their laps and knock on their doors and get the support and caressing I want and need. Just knock and go for it!"

The quiet of my meditation time resumes. Then an insight comes, a connection. With it a wave of tender awareness, followed by soft tears. I get a sense that Star-Thrower sent Bastet over the moment I began seeking communication. She brings a message from the Stars. "I'm here, I'm in attendance, I'm your faithful companion and comfort on your way." I become aware that this has happened on a number of occasions but I did not get the message until now. My heart feels so wide open.

I prepare myself for a visit to the chemotherapy doctor, Dr. Tellez. I write out a list of questions. I want to know: What does chemo do? How does it work? Why did I react so sensitively? How do they know the appropriate dosage for people like me? What if I develop symptoms again? And more. I ask my friend Patti who works across the street from the doctor's office building if she could meet me there and be a support for me. I feel the need for an extra pair of ears to listen and help me get the information I want.

Dr. Tellez is kind and takes time. I show her my drawings, especially #13 where I feel so terrible. She has liked my drawings all along.

She makes sure I ask every question on my list and that I feel satisfied with the answers. We have an agreement that I will call her every three days to report on how I feel. If I begin to have ulcers, I will call her immediately. We can go off chemo anytime it becomes too much. But, she promises, if I can handle it, the chemotherapy really supports the radiation process.

INITIATION DAY 50, FEELING PEACEFUL

Drawing 14 comes during this peaceful week. My joy of living comes back. I spend time in nature just listening, watching and healing. Finally I can draw a face that looks older, but a bit gray. I want to find a colored pen that will make my flesh look more real.

I look at last week's picture, Drawing 13, and remember how much pain and abandonment I felt. My fears said it would get worse, but it has not. My profound connection with the Friend is back, and that is so essential for me.

Star-Seer, can you feel your life force flowing fully? Flowing more fully than ever before in your life? Enjoy the J1ow, it's like a tingly charge, it's as though all your cells are dancing, can you feel it?

It's as though a rainbow fountain at your core is splashing vibrant life from some inexhaustible place. Secret smiles and ready laughter are the norm, bubbling up from a joyous source. You now see everything as gift.

Everything in this moment is alive with wonder, sparkling with freshness. Kindness and gentle actions hide around each door you walk through, each person you observe! Enlightenment is what you are experiencing but do not become involved with words and labels. They are poor conveyors of a profound experience.

INITIATION DAY 54, A CONVERSATION WITH A DOCTOR

"Dr. Keil, I'm a sore ass!"

"It really hurts?" "Yes."

"Well, I've heard many people describe themselves in many ways, but I've never heard your description before—are you using the suppositories and gel?"

"Yes, they really help."

"That's all you can do right now."

"Just bear it? I'm bleeding a lot all of a sudden."

"When the tumor leaves, it leaves an ulcer. That's probably what's bleeding."

"Oh! That certainly reframes everything for me! I thought my bowels were disintegrating."

"No, not at all."

"Only 10 more days of chemo and radiation!"

"Yes."

PAIN MANAGEMENT

A big side effect of the radiation is the burning of the sensitive tissues at my root chakra, the bladder, vagina, and especially the lower bowel and anus. As these tissues are burned repeatedly with the continuous radiation, they develop fissures, they swell, get raw, red and feverish. Combine that with the fact that the side effects of chemotherapy make problems too. My digestive track cannot hold anything. It can't process food much anymore. All it wants to do is cramp and push everything on through. Clearly I must stay close to a bathroom.

If I go out, it can only be for maybe 45 minutes. I go where there is a bathroom handy and then I wear a pad (I used to laugh at the names of some of those products like "Serenity" and "Depends" lining the walls of the pharmacy. Now I know that serenity is what I want to depend on! I also bring a towel and a washcloth in a baggie. I have these things in my car and in my purse all the time. Accidents and near accidents are a common occurrence.

There is no warning, I just explode and when I do, my sore tissues send pain and distress messages with a stinging that goes on and on. It's so sharp that sometimes all I can do is to be possessed by it, going into it and into it and into it. I make myself take deep breaths and maybe groan ohhhhh a bit. Soon it all passes until the next time. I am learning to let the pain have its way. The pain demands that I be present and mindful. I am learning to let it hurt and hurt while I stay with it, not fight it, not be mad at it, not wish it wasn't here, just be attentive for as long as it lasts.

I have learned not to be distracted by outside stimulation, like trying to talk on the phone at the same time. I learned not to leave the bathroom before all the pain has gone just because a friend is visiting and I want to resume our conversation. Then the pain becomes overwhelming and I get teary and emotional.

I realize that when I try to do something else during my explosion times I am resisting being with the pain and it does not like that. The pain seems to want me to listen to it. Take it seriously. Attend to it. So, I stay with my process and take lots of time alone. Then I can be with the pain when it comes.

My friends learn that when an explosion comes I hang up and run, no time for explanations. Most of the time I do not answer the phone anymore. I listen to my messages and return calls as I feel able. I have begun putting a brief health bulletin on my voice mail, as well as a message thanking people for their kind thoughts and prayers.

INITIATION DAY 55, THE END OF THE TUNNEL

I begin to feel I am at the end of a long journey. I am like an exhausted runner who sees the finishing line just ahead. It reminds me of some of the challenging treks I have taken. There was the long trek in the Himalayas; the shining trail high in the Andes. There were trips of several weeks each trekking in the bushveld of Africa, camping where lions roamed at night and elephants tore trees down for dinner nearby. The treks were sometimes hard, pushing my friends and me almost beyond our limits.

There were times when we were in danger, like when the cape buffalo charged us because we rounded a rocky wall and surprised him. Or when we were walking a narrow ledge and feeling dizzy at 13,000 feet. Sometimes we were in pain, sick, exhausted, but we pushed on and the prize was worth it all. The prize of breaking out of our too civilized ways and finding our place in the family of life. The prize of seeing nature at her most noble and volatile. The prize of facing danger and overcoming.

There is light at the end of the tunnel in my cancer therapy process and I can see it. I begin Drawing 15 using the tunnel image. Looking beyond the tunnel I can sense a new dawn is coming. I will never lose sight of the fact that the tunnel itself was filled with gifts and goodness so I put in the rainbow colors.

I still have my chemo pack but in about a week it will come off and I will move freely again. I have more radiation treatments but I feel that it has been worth it because now Herald has transmuted from killer rage to compassionate action. One of the rewards of being cleansed from that old pattern is feeling a release of new energy coursing up and down my spine.

As I consider the end of this part of my Initiation, I feel good. There were some difficult times, I would say about 10% was hard, the rest more than manageable, even though I call myself a sore ass now!

I have an epiphany this morning. My heart floods with thanks to my son and all that I learned from my relationship with him. I was brought to my knees, overwhelmed by grief and have come to a new place of liberation as a result. I ask that he be blessed wherever he is. Just bless him and send 1,000 angels to guide and comfort him.

June 8 '00
Initiation Day 55
Chemo/Radiation
over soon.
A new day
dawns...
I can
feel it!
15.

INITIATION DAY 58, WHAT DO I BRING?

Dear Star-Thrower, you bring me so much. You carry me across the turbulent stream like that Persian art on the Rumi poetry card. You advise me; bless me; comfort me. Tell me, what do I bring to you?

That is my question this morning.

Star-Seer, that's some of what you give me. You are beginning to recognize me, to break through to the truth about me and bust wide open those lies and horror stories' people tell about me.

Remember how it hurt when people did not see who you really were and spread rumors and bad stories? Well, is it not a wondrous relief when the real you is acknowledged? That's what Hafiz gave me, that's what you are giving me!

There is so much more. The joy of watching you gain your freedom. The pleasure of watching you stretch out and fill more of the template of your possibilities. Yes, you are expanding and becoming more of who you truly are!

Multiply your joy as you watched your daughter, Sarah, become more fully herself and overcome some obstacles in her life and you will get the point I am trying to make. I receive joy in watching you break free, embrace life and become more of what I know you to be.

Star-Thrower, I am awed by all the dynamics, the preparations, the synchronicities of this Initiation. In fact, I am awed that you really care that much for the emotional block in me, just one person. I can hardly believe the infinite patience and measureless care that were used in planning all the details of this Initiation.

Dear one, this event, this Initiation, is not just a careless little happening. It is key to your reason for taking on life. Hosts beyond are cheering for you, can you believe this? It is a new day for you. All the dynamics of your life are now different as you have made a new peace with your past and your family legacy. Stay mindful and you will see what it's like living in this land of magic.

Yes, I'm throwing a wild party in your heart these days and ever so many dear Beings who sing and dance and laugh are filling every corner with music. Can you hear the music? Are you tapping your toes to the beat?

INITIATION DAY 59, HAFIZ AND HIS POETRY

I feel a profound sense of awe when I read the poems from the fourteenth century poet, Hafiz. The radiance of his great heart shines through and lights my heart. Though little known in the western world, Hafiz is the most treasured poet of Persia with over 600 poems to his credit. The message of Hafiz is full of relevance for today for he offers wild love songs from God to us. Thus we gain courage, and hope as we dare to believe we can grow closer to the Friend, to freedom, to our own divine Self.

The renderings of these poems came through Daniel Ladinsky in two little volumes. One is *I HEARD GOD LAUGHING.* The other is *THE SUBJECT TONIGHT IS LOVE.* Landinsky doesn't know this and I keep meaning to write and tell him, but I am a grateful, grateful reader of these works.

A fragrance in Landinsky's work tells of the high quality of his relationship with his own heart and the Beloved, the Friend. The care and love with which Landinsky treats these poems that he passes on to us encourages us to catch something of the brilliance, the tender and playful facets of God. And without quite realizing what is happening, we find ourselves transformed. I find I can only absorb a little at a time, then I must pause and feel the profound nourishment I have been offered.

Drawing 16 comes from the poem *In A Tree House* that I quoted from in Drawing 12 as well. This verse goes like this:

God conducts the affairs
of the whole universe
while throwing wild parties
on a tree limb
in your heart.

In the drawing I adapted the wording slightly to personalize it.

I spend a lot of time quietly and alone. I enjoy watching the trees dance in the summer breezes. I love the birds feasting and squabbling at the feeder.

June 12 '00
Invitation Day 59

Star Throwers
Conducts
the
organs
of
the
whole
uni-
verse
while
throwing
wild
parties
on a tree
limb in
my heart.

adapted from Hafiz's
poem

16

INITIATION DAY 60, CODEINE HAS COME!

"Oh, how I love Codi, Oh how I love Codi…" This is my new song. Codeine has made my life mellow and though I know our relationship is short-lived, I am grateful for her presence this last week. The pain is there even with Codeine. I hate to imagine what it might be like without. Drawing 17 shows how Codeine becomes a hallelujah chorus permeating the pain.

In spite of my complaints, I feel my body strong and resilient. I am not at my edge by any means. I feel I have wonderful reserves to call on if needed. I pay attention to what my body needs; I sleep a lot; I rest a lot. I only see people who give me energy and avoid those who take it. I limit my phone conversations. Most people understand my need to save all my energy for healing.

I have flashes of insight showing that my ancestors on my mother's side are aware of what I am transmuting and cheer me on. My great grandmother, Jane, my grandmother Philemenna and mother Ruth, along with her sisters, Virginia and Margaret. They all live in the timeless now, so what I do liberates them in their parallel universe. I resonate with the Native American teaching that what we do in this life has profound effects reaching back 7 generations, and forward 7 generations. The Bible speaks of this dynamic as well, 'The sins of the fathers are visited on to the children unto the 3rd and 4th generations.'

A DEAR FRIEND COMES

My dear friend, Titia Ellis, comes today from her home in Santa Fe. She is the one who introduced me to Hafiz, sending me a book of poems shortly after my 'Great Friend' experience in December. Titia is coming to be with me for this last difficult week of therapy.

I find it a challenge to set aside the 'host' role. However, I listen to my friends as they remind me that it is my time to receive and there is nothing I need to do to make sure Titia will have a nice time. This is another lesson in 'receiving.'

Titia's whole focus was to support me. She listened to me, answered my phone, accompanied me to my treatments, cheered me up, did dishes and a hundred other things. Her presence in itself was enough to make me feel better.

Titia also came as a member of a Charitable Trust board for which I am responsible. Patti Slama is our incredible executive director. It is a privilege to be able to make grants. Worthy and talented people have visions for a kinder more just world, but they need financial help. Because we are a small Trust we can take risks and provide seed money for start-up projects. Then when the new organizations have have worked through some of the kinks and established a track record, they can go the big foundations.

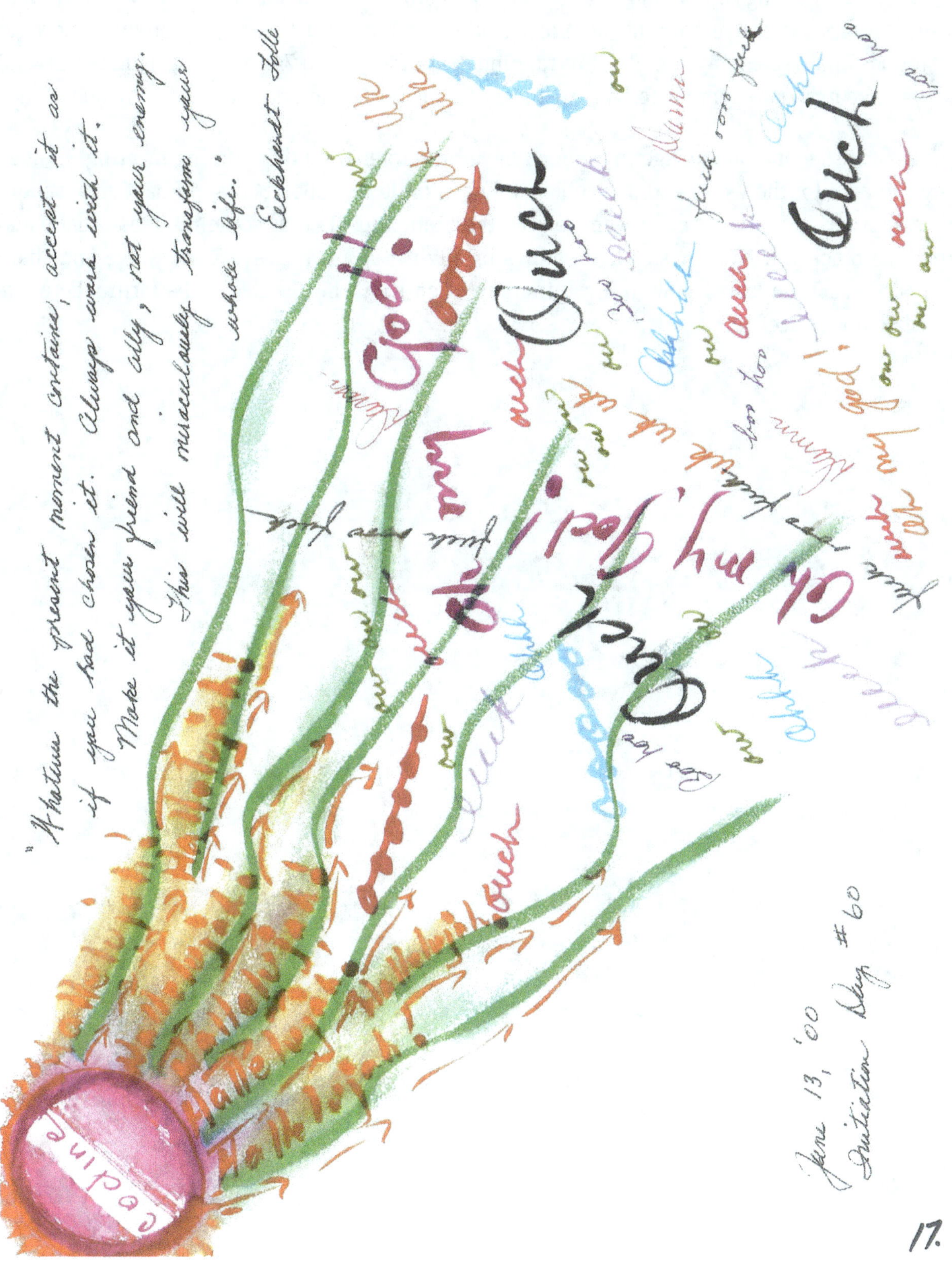

We have three meetings a year and this is the weekend for one. As a board we have worked together for seven years. After overcoming some difficulties we moved to a place of profound respect and love for one another. There are eight of us ranging in age from 32 to 74. We bring delicious diversity that we have grown to appreciate. We trust group decisions as far superior to any by one of us.

Cancer has brought a big change in me for I have little interest in this coming meeting. I have no energy to care for the world and its problems. I need to be self-absorbed and I have to accept that this is appropriate. I do not even want to read the grant appeals that come in, a task that usually brings me much joy. I will visit the meetings briefly to say hi, feel everyone's love and share a bit about what I am learning with my Initiation. Then I will head back to the farm where I feel nourished and peaceful.

CHAPTER SIX

STAR-THROWER VISITS AGAIN

You have been invited to meet
The Friend.

No one can resist a Divine Invitation.

That narrows down all our choices
To just two:

We can come to God
Dressed for Dancing,

Or

Be carried on a stretcher
To God's Ward.

Hafiz

INITIATION DAY 63, IT'S OVER!

On the top of a new page in my journal, I write in large colorful letters, IT'S OVER! With my dear and loyal friends Titia and Marianne as witnesses, I enjoy the removal of my chemo pack. Then I complete my last radiation treatment. I am euphoric. I can not stop smiling! It's as if I have run the triathlon and crossed the finishing line. I am finished! I am free!

I dream my first night after completion:

I am out with friends and we are carefully climbing smooth rocks by the sea in a place of such beauty it reminds me of the Norwegian Fjords. We are careful not to slip off as there is a bit of snow on everything.

I go ahead of the others and down a little. Suddenly, a huge fish, maybe 4 or 5 feet long, comes partly out of the sea. Propping itself on its fins on the rock just below me, it looks directly into my eyes for a long, long time.

It's eyes are placed so they can see straight ahead. They are dark with gold, brown, red and green flecks and lights in them.

I am transfixed. It slips back into the sea. Next thing I know rising in front of a cliff the Great Fish leaps maybe 100 feet into the air before splashing back into the sea and disappearing.

I know a very special, magical, intelligent Being came to me. A gift from the sea!

I find J.E. Cirlot's *The Dictionary of Symbols* and read that fish are a symbol of profound life and of the spiritual world that lies under the world of appearances. The fish represents the life-force surging up. Fish are mystic and psychic animals that live in water. They are a symbol of dissolution, renovation, and regeneration.

The dream said it all. I am entering a new time of profound life. My life-force is surging up after that old pattern dissolved and renovation and regeneration is taking its place. Drawing 18 depicts my gift from the sea—but does not do the absolutely mesmerizing Great Fish justice.

INITIATION DAY 67, OHHHHH MY ASS, MY POOR ASS.

I am at the farm and I have come to realize I must stop taking codeine, the side effects are getting too costly. I will not go into how painful and difficult the next 10 days were. Suffice it to say I was house bound. I got a few messages from Star-Thrower but mostly I just lay on the couch or on my bed (I could not sit very well). I looked out at the trees and the clouds. At night, I watched the stars.

Dear one, I know this is a difficult time.

Star-Thrower, yes, this is a hard part of my process. Will I ever heal? How much more pain? What can I do to help the healing process?

June 16, 2000
Radiation Day 63
Dream: "A gift from the sea."
Chemo and Radiation over

Star-Seer, one step at a time. Right now, this minute, it is only mildly uncomfortable, right? Have no expectations here, just stay with your process. You have time and space for what you need. Patience, dear one, all is well, all is so well.

At that point, I look out the window and see a pair of mourning doves. They are a favorite bird of mine and I had not spotted any on the farm as yet. I had quizzed my neighbors but they, not as obsessed with doves as I, had not noticed. I have had mourning dove sightings all around the world from Africa to England, from Nepal to Peru. They are like a mystical symbol for me. If I had a family crest, one of the symbols would be a pair of mourning doves.

In 1993 when I lived in a townhouse in Chicago, a pair of mourning doves made a nest in my open bedroom window. My husband was dying at the time and the gift of these birds cannot be overestimated. They built their nest and shared their duties equally as they sat on their eggs and raised their 3 offspring. I documented it all with my camera. Now, here they are on the first day of summer, June 21, sitting on my deck railing and eyeing the bird feeder. Seeing those doves when I am in so much pain and wondering if I will ever heal, becomes a tangible beacon of hope.

There are other signs like the butterfly on my bathroom window. In the midst of pain when I use the bathroom so often-the sign of transformation is there, on that window, resting, wings open to the warm sun. I am reminded of the transformation taking place through perhaps the most humble part of my body. What a lesson, every part of the body is sacred. Every part is necessary and holy.

I do Drawing 19 and I like it. I am through the tunnel but there are some unexpected thorn trees to negotiate. The new day is surely dawning. Star-Thrower is there. Magenta's ever present care is clear and I am OK, even though my fanny hurts and hurts!

INITIATION DAY 69, IT WASN'T OVER!!!!

Expectations break down. This week's experience was painful, hard, worrisome, unexpected.

I had fancied myself healing quickly after therapy ended. I expected to catch up on all the tasks I put off all these weeks, like gardening, getting the porch furniture I so wanted, walking in the woods and so forth. Instead I am just trying to survive one moment at a time, one stinging attack at a time—and they happen so often—what is going on inside me?

Lofty thoughts and intoxicating spiritual heights have fled. Instead I ponder the miracle of my digestive system and how nice when it works well. I pay attention to my pain, I focus, feel, surrender. I am forever putting ointments on my fanny. I am so greasy I carry a towel with me so I do not ruin furniture with grease spots when I sit or lie! I change my clothes several times a day and my wash is almost as much as when there is a new baby in the house.

Dear one, remember you are in a healing process that many have trodden successfully before you. Remember too that Herald has transmuted through this process. He is gone. His message was delivered, heeded, and acted on. You are forever changed.

The slow plodding steps are part of the process. You must learn to walk the tedious times and harvest the subtle gifts awaiting you there, gifts like a sense of being, not doing. Gifts like a sense of your essential value even when you are just resting, feeling blue, too blah to think positively, too blah to reach out to anyone.

INITIATION DAY 73, YES! I AM HEALING!

I feel better. A little strength is returning. I am able to live a bit more normally as my bowels do not explode quite as often. I have turned a major corner. I even risk going to Lowe's to buy a hammock for my courtyard garden area. It is my first foray into life in about ten days and I find the traffic loud and the store confusing. However a nice young person helps me and I bring my hammock home. I even put it together.

Star-Thrower keeps reminding me that I am doing well and I am to concentrate on the love that is all around me. This will make my heart light and speed my healing. I go to bed grateful that I am sleeping well.

I awaken and look at the clock. It is almost midnight. I feel the urge to get up and look at the sky. It is a clear moonless night and the sky is alive with stars.

Getting a comforter and pillow, I head for my new hammock. Snuggling down, I hear a soft call from behind the screen door, Bastet, my cat, wants to come out too. Zeus, my other cat stays curled up on my bed deep in sleep. Now the cat and I snuggle in the comforter. I gaze up at the sky and marvel. There are so many stars shinning brightly that it is hard to pick out the familiar constellations.

Suddenly a streak across the midnight sky, a shooting star, trailing sparkles that make a long, long tail. It stretches from directly overhead and down into the southern horizon disappearing behind the courtyard fence. It is the largest display I have ever witnessed.

Yes! Yes! Star Thrower wanted me to see this display. Yes! This is a confirmation of our relationship. What a tender, awesome gift; a gift that speaks deeply to my heart.

MORE GIFTS

The June night is filled with fireflies. Like celestial popcorn in some gigantic grate, they pop their tiny lights all over the meadows and by the tall trees making up the edge of the forest. Some of them fly so high they look like winking stars, stars above, stars all around.

Meanwhile, the wetlands behind my house are laughing. Seriously, they are laughing! Ho ho ho ho's fill the night air. The frogs whose turn it is to sing noware so funny. They have a ho ho chortle that they give back and forth. Some pitched higher, some lower. They all use about 4 ho ho's in a row. One lazy low voice can only muster three slow ho's. It is as if the entire night is laughing and dancing with joy. Can life be any better than this?

When I finish Drawing 20, I realize the series is complete. I have not felt the urge to draw since, instead that creative energy has gone into writing this story. A story I hope brings you comfort, hope, and assurance that your process is guided by a great love and though there will be hard times, you are not alone. Miracles will attend your way whether you heal into more life on this earth, or you heal into life in another dimension.

INITIATION DAY 77, THIS BOOK BEGINS

Dear Star-Thrower, I feel that my series of pictures is complete with your visitation on June 27. What do you think? Is it time to gather together my experience in a book form? Will this be helpful for others?

Dear Star-Seer, yes, as it feels ripe in you, begin to organize your experience and have fun! Let it be an expression of your joy and of our Jove and of our heart's desire to lighten the load for others entering a similar initiation!

Continue to watch your life and see all the gifts coming your way. Isn't this a delightful way to live? Watching for gifts of Jove coming your way?

A GIFT FROM MOTHER

My sister, Sylvia, has been so attentive sending flowers, gifts, checking on me, praying for me, encouraging me. Today, her high school teaching year over, she drives from her home in Michigan for a visit. I am resting on my towel on the couch when I hear her voice: "Hello Paula, I bring you a gift from Mother…."

I burst into tears, a gift from mother, gone over 23 years. A gift from mother. What could it be? I can't stop weeping. A gift from mother....

Mother loved to raise African violets. When she died, Sylvia took one and nurtured it all these years. As a gift for me, she separated out a plant and put it in a crisp, white pot. The violet is blooming with little clusters of delicate white flowers edged in purple.

A gift from mother.

Do we ever get over our deep need for mother? For the one who cares unconditionally? The one whom we needed so desperately as we came into the world and the one who (experience and hospice nurses tell me) we call for as we leave?

A gift from mother.

I have felt the women in my ancestral line watching me and cheering me on during this "pattern breaking" Initiation in which they had been caught: Jane, Philemenna, Ruth.

Sylvia also brought me little frozen meals of the kind of food my sensitive stomach could handle. She is gifted in the home arts, and she loves doing it.

A CHALLENGE COMES ON INITIATION DAY 85

How easily fear is triggered as I see the various doctors for checkups. There is good news! Upon examination, it appears Herald has transmuted and in his place is healthy tissue. Yes!!!!

However, Dr. Kiel, the radiation oncologist, informs me it is time to schedule the surgery for the middle of August. "But," I sputter, "what if the cancer is gone, what if all the tests next week show that I am cancer free, I do not want the surgery then."

Dr. Kiel, bless her heart, spent a lot of time citing statistics and studies that indicate the best course of action is to have the surgery anyway. Confused and resistant, my eyes get moist. Her resident passes me the tissues. I know Dr. Kiel sees tragic cases every day of people whose cancer returns and I feel her wanting the best for me. She makes her point so eloquently and intelligently that I leave with all my fears triggered.

Dear Star-Seer, I am watching you with all your lists of pro's and con's regarding the decision you are facing. Dear one, your heart knows what is right, your body feels what it wants, your soul knows its truth and its journey. Only your mind is confused.

I promise to send you so many messages that you will have no doubt about my guidance, no doubt at all! You already know, don't you? You just want reassurance as Gideon did in the Old Testament story. Because, like Gideon you are doing something unusual, something that experts would say is foolish. This is an exercise in putting your life on the line for what you deeply feel is right for you.

I know you. You are afraid because what you deeply know is right for you is also the 'easier' way and the easier way, by definition, is the 'way to hell and all things bad.' The 'good' way is hard, rugged, and therefore by virtue of all that suffering more worthy of a blessing, a reward. No pain, no gain. Still appeasing angry gods?

OK, that's a pattern that can go too, a belief system whose usefulness (if there ever was a good use for it) is past. I Jove you, you are so dear to me.

WHAT HAPPENS AFTER MY FIRST DRINK IN THREE MONTHS?

I did not sleep well last night as the dire warnings of Dr. Kiel spun around in my head and the burden of a decision was on my mind. It's been a beautiful day in Chicago and now a sunny warm evening. I decide to mix myself a gin and tonic, my favorite summer drink and my first in a long time. Sitting by the big windows overlooking the lake and the sky, I get an idea. What if my three closest friends would come next weekend for a 'discernment house party?' I trust their intuition and I trust the heightened wisdom that is available when we four are together.

Patty Woerner, Titia Ellis, Marianne Johnson and I have been closer than sisters for years, meeting several times a year for 4 or 5 days in each other's homes. There is nothing we cannot discuss. We share our spiritual journeys. We meditate together. We discuss money, sex, aging, life, children, mates, health and more.

We have trekked in the remotest part of Africa sleeping under the southern cross. We have traveled 44 hours during monsoon season to spend time in the presence of his Holiness the Dalal Lama in Dharamsala, India. We have snorkeled in the Aegean Sea among the sponges and bright darting fish. We count on one another. I also count their husbands as among my closest friends. What if these women would come and help me discern what my next step should be, surgery or not? I'll call them right now.

I have to say, I think the alcohol gave me the courage to ask for this favor. I do not know if the idea would have even come to my normal mind.

A MESSAGE FROM HERALD

I see a gifted medical intuitive and body energy worker, Kurt Hill, each week. Last Thursday as I lay on the massage table, I asked him to see if he could get any guidance for me regarding what my body needs. Is there is any cancer left? Do I need the radical surgery scheduled for August 15?

Kurt is silent. I can tell he is going deep. When he comes back he says "Paula, your body is so open right now, it is easy to get a message. I don't see you having surgery August 15. It wouldn't hurt you, but your body doesn't need it. Your cancer is gone."

A few minutes pass and Kurt gets a "hit." I can tell because there is this little grunt. "Herald is gone, he likes his new form and he just wanted you to know that!"

I laugh! I love that message. Herald likes his new form! He is gone and he likes his new form!

CHAPTER SEVEN

JELLY SIDE UP

A WALK

My eyes already touch the sunny hill,
going far ahead of the road I have begun.
So we are grasped by what we cannot grasp;
it has its inner light, even from a distance--

and changes us, even if we do not reach it,
into something else, which, hardly sensing it, we already are;
a gesture waves us on, an answering our own wave...
but what we feel is the wind in our faces.

Rainer Maria Rilke

I AM GRASPED BY WHAT I CANNOT GRASP

I feel like a new creation, I wrote in my journal on July 12, Initiation day 89. I feel freer from old torments and hungers and that accusing, needling voice that wouldn't leave me alone. I feel freer to express myself, put myself out there without trying to be perfect.

Just take my drawings, for example. They are crude, unsophisticated and all that. Yet I know they carry a story that needs to be told and so I am willing to appear the fool and put it out there. If it doesn't touch anyone, well, what have I lost? I loved the process itself. And, if Spirit wants to use my efforts to help others, that's great too. It's not up to me. I don't need to be heard like I did with my first book. This work comes from a different place inside me.

Star-Thrower, do you have anything you want to say to me at this time?

Dear Star-Seer, I think you have summed up your process very well. I have enjoyed watching your excitement and energy for this project. I know your joy when you give yourself to a creative endeavor.

Let me tell you a little secret. This project of yours will continue to flow and effortlessly move to completion. Watch how the way just opens before you.

By effortlessly I don't mean you won't work hard, but I mean you WANT to work at it. It fulfills you, brings you joy. It helps you integrate your experience on many levels. It is rewarding. In a way, you are playing now. You aren't trying to prove anything, you are just being you and as real as you know how to be. Bravo!

IS HERALD REALLY GONE? TWO MORE TESTS

It is Friday, July 21 and Initiation Day 98. I have two tests. There is an ultra sound in the morning and a CT scan in the afternoon. It is important to check where Herald used to be. A bit nervous, I prepare. No food, just clear juices. Then I give myself two enemas, an hour apart, to clean things up for the ultra sound.

The doctor performing my ultra sound is a favorite of mine, Dr. Vanagunas. Northwestern Hospital has just purchased new ultra sound equipment, more sophisticated than the equipment used on me just three months ago. Everyone in the department is impressed with the improvements.

Soon, in living color, on the TV-like monitor, is my lighted up, highly magnified, inner tissue (notice I avoid saying rectum!). Because of Herald's position I do not even need drugs to put me in a twilight zone for this procedure. Dr. Vanagunas searches for Herald, if not Herald, then a bit of scar indicating where he was. All we see is healthy tissue with a web of tiny blood vessels creating a beautiful pattern. I realize I am gaining increasing respect for the miracle of my body and all its intricate systems.

Finally, we see a red spot, greatly magnified. It is the size and color of a pencil eraser tip. "Ah, that's where Herald was," Dr. Vanagunas says, "now we'll look at the layers of the bowel wall to see if any cancer lurks there." He checks all five layers and all looked healthy. The nurse and doctor congratulate me on my good news!

My faithful friend, Jackie, was waiting for me. She looks up from her reading as I enter the waiting room. I raise my hand in a gesture of victory and proclaim loudly for all to hear "Yes! Yes! All is well!" She jumps up from the chair and we hug. Then she grabs her camera and takes a picture of my victory moment!

BREAK THE RULES!

Jackie and I now head for my CT Scan. "I knew it, Paula, I knew all along that you would come through this and Herald would transmute!"

The nurse takes me to a changing room and gives me a thin green hospital gown. The air conditioning is on full blast. It is cold. I exercise my new skills and decide to take care of myself in spite of 'rules.' Why should I be cold, sitting for an hour, drinking the cold barium, without anything on but a thin skimpy cotton gown?

So, I put my hospital gown on over my clothes. There are about 6 or 7 women waiting for a scan in the drinking room, all shivering. The nurse brings white, cotton blankets and the women eagerly take them. Now there is a room full of white mummies—and me.

When it is time for the scan, I just slip off my pants, put them in my commodious purse and lie down on the scan board. Immediately I request a blanket as it is cold here too. I say all this to encourage you readers to consider your needs and break the rules if necessary to get them met! I cannot emphasize this enough. Take good care of yourself along the way.

INITIATION DAY 100 AND THE 'DISCERNMENT HOUSE PARTY'

It is Sunday and my friends arrive for our 'discernment house party.' Patty Woerner flies in from New Hampshire, Titia Ellis came a few days early from an Island in Canada where her family gathers every summer, and Marianne Johnson who lives close to me.

I am getting my wish. It would not be happening if I had not dared (after the courage a gin and tonic provided) to ask! When talking to Patty on the phone about the arrangements, I thanked her for her efforts on my behalf. I also confessed that I felt a bit unworthy of all this attention. She responded: "Paula, have you considered that it feels good to be asked?" Hummmm, something to think about!

There are no words to describe the feeling of being in the midst of friends who know each other well and love profoundly. All of us went back to school in midlife for advanced degrees and began new careers after child rearing. Our time together is full of laughter and light-hearted bantering as we pitch in with kitchen duties and household chores. Tears are welcome too and come often—

sometimes mixed with laughter. There are times when we hardly know which we are doing.

The weather is unseasonably cool and since no one brought warm enough clothes I dig among my winter things and pull out outfits from pajamas to jackets. Titia and I love to sleep under the stars, so we inflate some mattresses and drag every available blanket out to the deck. Titia has a rule that she won't go to sleep until she has seen a falling star.

There is an understanding of the special gifts each of us has. Also, the sensitive spots each of us carries—wounds that must be acknowledged and treated with compassion.

I had ordered the latest research and journal articles on colorectal cancer and its treatment from Health Resource, Inc. These trained people access the web, check medical journals and current research. They organize and package relevant materials, shipping them within a few days. Both mainline treatments and alternative therapies are covered as well as the names of treatment facilities here and abroad. This material proved helpful as I educated myself. My women friends scanned it to educate themselves as well.

On Monday morning, we meditate together, asking for guidance. I wrote to Star-Thrower during our quiet time: I glory in this circle of friends gathered from afar to be here with me now. Friends who know spirit, who are on the path of the drum beat coming from the depth of the stars.

Take us to the next level. Guide us to where you want us to go. Open our eyes of deep seeing and our ears of soul. The 'us' part is the grace, like a fragrant oil. It is the 'us' that helps our gears turn and our rigid places move again.

Star-Seer, we glory in your circle with you. It is circles like yours that create the space where my liberating energies can come through, where my laughter can be heard and the comforts I Jong to give are given.

Patty (a Presbyterian minister) wrote a message for me: '"Go out in joy (from Isaiah).' You have found joy, you have already lightened up. In making your decision, the shamanic principles apply here 'do not be dependent on outcome.' Go bravely into the unknown, grounded in reality. A little anxiety is good, this means you are realistic and human. We all die, so the question is, what risks do you choose? And a guide for all of life is to live confidently--never really knowing!"

The consensus from my dear friends was that I did not need the radical surgery unless some disturbing new news came to light.

Patty asked a question. "Paula, you look so radiant now, so healthy. How did you look during your treatment time? I didn't see you as the others did... in fact I felt left out." I shrugged and turned the question to Marianne and Titia. Suddenly Marianne burst into tears. "She was so sick. I was so concerned for her. It was hard to watch. I didn't know it hurt me so much until now." Titia also cried, her tears expressing her love for me and her pain for what I went through. "Paula, you are our teacher now. What we are learning as we watch you is so important."

That night as I pondered all these things, my mind turned to my friends and the power of their love for me. The deep way they carried me in their hearts and bodies. In fact, I am impressed over how many people 'carried' me during this time, from my little great niece Gwen who prayed for me every night, to my busy lawyer who just called to see how I was and said I was in his prayers. Even Jean Houston, head of Mystery School where I am a student, called from New York to pray with me over the phone—a powerful prayer session that left me shaking! So many people were part of my Initiation. I did not do it alone! I was carried.

TEST RESULTS AND THE SURGEON

July 26, Initiation Day103, I have an appointment to see the surgeon. Dr. Stryker came highly recommended. He is tops in his field. The walls of his office are filled with diplomas, awards, and recognition's of excellence.

In our first meeting, I liked him. I felt I had a real ally in my search for healing. "Paula, I think I can save your rectum so you won't have to have a colostomy for the rest of your life. I'll do a good job for you!" And, I knew he would.

"I couldn't have hoped for anything better than these test results, Paula. Your tumor is 95% gone! (Ninety-five percent gone? No! I know it's 100% gone!) Now let's talk about the surgery…."

"Dr. Stryker, if all the tests say no cancer is found, why would I want the surgery?"

"You can never tell when little clusters of cancer cells remain, too small for the tests to pick up. The only safe thing to do is the surgery. We need to see the lymph nodes in that area and take them out. Even if we find you didn't have any cancer, you can have peace of mind. This is the perfect time for you. When patients have the radiation you had, there is a period of 4 or 5 months before scar tissue forms, making surgery more difficult. After that time, we would have to give you a bag (colostomy)."

"Right now I am concerned about a handsome man in his forties who just came to me. After his radiation and chemotherapy, all tests indicated, like yours, that his cancer was gone. So he told his doctors, 'I feel great, the tests say the cancer is gone, I do not want the surgery.' Three months passed and all was still clear. Six months passed, same. His nine month check-up showed spots on his liver. Then he came to me. We had to do the radical surgery plus a procedure putting chemo directly into his liver. He missed his window of opportunity. I do not want you to do the same. Look at you, you're healthy, this surgery would give you 10, 15, 20 more years. Are you afraid of it or what?"

"No, I just don't think I need it. I feel I'm cancer free. You know, Dr. Stryker, I am more than a body, I am a mind, emotions, and spirit. I have worked with my cancer on all these levels. I have had many indications that I don't need the radical surgery."

There is a pause. He puts his head in his hands, rubs his eyes. I know I have disappointed the doctor. He sees so many tragic cases, and spends his time doing everything he can to save lives. I know he wants the best for me. All his experience says I am making a mistake.

"OK, there is another procedure, its like a deep biopsy. It means only about 2 days in the hospital and a week recovery. I would go in through the anus, locate the scar where the tumor was and take out all the layers of the bowel underneath. After sewing you up, the tissue would go to a lab for testing. If the lab finds any cancer cells, would you have the surgery then?"

"Oh my God, yes! Of course!"

On my way out of the office as I reschedule things with Kimberly, the doctor's able assistant, he joins us. "About two months ago, after you were already in therapy, Northwestern acquired new scanning equipment called PET Scan. We are currently testing the accuracy of this scanner in detecting cancer. When patients come in they are given a scan before treatment followed by radiation and chemotherapy as usual. Then they have another scan before surgery. We want to find out if the scanner's reports concur with what we see in surgery. If we can depend on the scan, we can find those people whose cancer is cured by the radiation and chemotherapy and we will know they do not need the surgery. This machine is far superior to anything we have now. Would you be willing to have a PET scan? The more information I can get, the better informed my decisions."

"Yes, oh yes, I'd like that!" So, it is arranged.

LEAVING THE DOCTOR'S OFFICE

I find I am full of adrenaline, even shaking a bit. I stop at a deli and get some salads for Patti Slama, Bill Johnson and myself. We have some Trust business to attend to, some checks to sign.

Waiting for Bill, I share with Patti my conversation with the surgeon. She hugs me. When Bill comes, he too understands why I am a charged up. "Paula, it takes so much energy to go up against a big system like the medical system...." My hand shakes a bit as I sign things. I can hardly wait to go back to the farm. There I can be quiet and sort my thoughts. There I can more easily listen to my deeper wisdom.

INITIATION DAY 104, BACK AT THE FARM

The first day back at the farm I cannot concentrate. All I want to do is clean the house after my wonderful house party. There are sheets to launder, dishes to wash, things to put back in place.

Then I see them. The mourning doves. I do not see them often, in fact the last time they visited was Initiation Day 68 when I wondered if the pain would ever go away. They were a sign that all was well then and they bring the same message now. They come together, male and female, landing on my roof and walking about. I take the sign to heart. All is well. All is well.

I am reminded of the message of Initiation Day 85 from StarThrower:

I promise to send you so many messages that you will have no doubt about my guidance, no doubt at all! You already know, don't you? You just want reassurance as Gideon did in the Old Testament story. Because, like Gideon you are doing something unusual, something that experts would say is foolish. This is an exercise in putting your life on the line for what you deeply feel is right for you.

INITIATION DAY 110, JELLY SIDE UP

What do I mean with my chapter title, Jelly Side Up? I mean that my life seems to be flowing. I have peace and patience where I used to be stressed. Things are working easily for me—even mistakes! If I drop my breakfast toast, it lands jelly side up! When I do a drawing and make a mess, somehow the mistake becomes part of the picture.

After meeting with nutritionist Sherry Belcher to plan a diet to support my bowel health, I realized I had gone past my parking meter time in downtown Chicago. Oh no, was my first thought, then out loud I said, I probably won't have a ticket as everything is jelly side up these days. I was right!

KISSING HERALD GOOD-BYE

I go see Dr. Martha Howard at Wellness Associates. We are putting together a plan to support my health and a cancer free life. I ask Martha if she has any thoughts about whether I need the deep biopsy procedure. She responds: "The decision is yours, Paula. But I see you as so happy and healthy now. You knew you needed to do the chemo/radiation. You had no doubts. Now, you aren't sure about more procedures. Surgery is so invasive, even this biopsy, to an area that has just been traumatized.

"One of the reasons statistics show a high rate of cancer returning is that people who have cancer go to a doctor, have medical interventions and then return to their former life just the way it was.

No diet change, no new health program in place, no emotional understanding, same problems at work, same relationship traumas. The mainline medical system doesn't teach the importance of changing your life. You, Paula, are changing your life!

"I've learned to trust my intuition (I interrupt and say that I still have a way to go on this one). I have seen over and over that I can trust a felt sense. I think you are clean. But I get a sense that Herald is still about in the air, wanting closure, wanting you to kiss him good-bye. Perhaps you could draw Herald this way, being kissed good-bye."

And so, Drawing 21 came into being. I loved doing it. It does seem like a fitting closure to our relationship—although Herald will never be forgotten!

The next day, Initiation day 110, I get my PET scan. It's a long tedious test where they put a radio active solution in your bloodstream. Cancer cells like this solution and gobble it up, I guess. As a result they light up. So then when the patient is scanned (which took 1 and 1/2 hours of not moving a muscle) it can pick up and record if and where there are cancer cells.

Although I have not gotten the official test results yet, the person in charge of the procedure said she hadn't seen anything to worry about and she gave me the thumbs up signal. As I leave the hospital, I sense this is the last procedure I will endure for a while.

MY HEALTH SUPPORT PROGRAM

Following are some of the changes I am making in my life. I share them not as prescriptions for you, but to give you a sense of what I am doing to change my life in healing ways. Some of these things I was already doing to some extent. I will focus on them more now.

1. Very important! I will spend time in quiet and solitude. I will meditate, journal, pay attention to my dreams, garden, simply listen to my life! I am still on sabbatical so I can spend a lot of time at the farm where I am close to nature.

2. I have changed my diet with the help of nutritionist Sherry Belcher and Dr. Howard. I am not doing macrobiotic or any other real stringent program, although those are really fine for some. I make fresh organic vegetable juice each day. I take CoQl0 along with other supplements. Each morning I take Missing Link, along with good oils like Barlean's Omega Twin. I take chlorophyll and I drink organic aloe vera juice made from the whole leaf. I am on an intestinal support intensive for a couple months to aid recovery and replace nutrients leached out by my therapies.

I will be on extra vitamin E for a while to keep scar tissue from forming as a result of radiation. I drink green tea daily. Hot in cool weather, iced in warm.

Of course I eat healthy foods and keep the junk and chocolates to a minimum (though they are still there at times—ummm). I use "The Ultimate Meal" a lot, it is excellent nutrition and easily absorbed in my system. Daily I cut up a fresh clove of garlic and take it, raw, with water. I think that's it for now.

3. I make sure I play and laugh. Funny movies are in. I see people with a sense of humor, people who give me life and energy. I seek small gatherings of well loved people. Good music I find healing, like the Chicago Symphony!

4. I really limit my time with people who take energy, no matter how well meaning they are. I limit my time in large crowds. I don't do cocktail parties anymore.

5. I don't do TV or the news much. Daily newspapers are out—too time consuming for me. Good books are in! (I'll let you in on a secret, I am a book-a-holic!) I enjoy good fiction, poetry, wisdom literature. I am reading the 4th in the Harry Potter series right now, all 700+ pages of it! I'm also reading *The Power of Now* by Eckhart Tolle. It's a book to ponder and re-read.

6. I explore ways to enjoy the outdoors while exercising. (I don't like gyms and exercise machines!) I am buying a kayak to reward myself for all I've been through! I want to enjoy rivers and lakes more. Mostly I walk, it's so convenient!

7. I still see marvelous Dr. Case at Universal Chiropractic and I'll have acupuncture every so often.

8. I have dreams I want to manifest. One dream is to build a thankyou 'labyrinth' on the farm. I love labyrinths and so I'll have a labyrinth party and we'll make one.

Oh, I forgot to say one exercise I do to overcome the effects of radiation. Maybe I'm a bit embarrassed to put it in print but my friends say I must.

Dr. Kiel, the radiation oncologist, warned that radiation can make sensitive vaginal tissues tighten and shrink. She gave me some vaginal dilators and surgical lubricant to use for a time to overcome these side effects of radiation. My 'discernment' group laughed as I brought out my new exercise equipment. Of course there were jokes. But I confessed to them that I find myself enjoying orgasms as rich as when I was much younger. Therapists all (Patty is both minister and therapist) they nodded knowingly and said, "Your life generating force has gained strength."

DR STRIKER AND I PART FRIENDS

I was a bit nervous when Dr. Striker asked me to come in to his office and sign something. Would he argue with my decision not to have any surgery, including the biopsy?

When I arrive, he comes to meet me shaking his finger playfully. I was relieved as he seems to be accepting my choice in a lighter way. Looking over my PET scan results, Dr. Stryker said it was all good news.

"I know I have disappointed you."

"No, it's just I want to be able to sleep nights. And your decision is not what I would have chosen for you."

"I know you want the best for me—I have really counted on you from our first meeting on."

"You're an intelligent woman and I know you understand your situation, you know what you're doing. But I want you to sign a statement, just for the record, that you are refusing the treatment I recommend."

"Sure, I'll be glad to do that."

He disappears for a few minutes and comes back with a handwritten statement. I sign with "Thank you Doctor" and my name.

I pull out Drawing 21 of me bidding Herald good-bye with kisses. I see the doctor get a little jolt as he looks at the images. He responds "This is what we hope for!"

"Doctor, how do I follow up? Come back in 6 months?"

"No, come see me in three months, I'll do a 10-minute examination... I need to sleep nights (there's that phrase again, he clearly cares!) I want to catch anything while I can still help you even though you might have a colostomy by then."

"OK, I'll be here!"

I left feeling like we were friends even though I didn't follow his advice. We respect each other and I will be glad to check in with him in 3 months.

MY LAST PARAGRAPH

Needless to say, I could go on and on. But it is time to close this book and get it out to you. I close with a message from StarThrower.

Dear one, I like the new picture. Herald feels honored, acknowledged, responded to. That is one of the endearing things about you. You take guidance and run with it, you always have.

I see you are noticing how happy the African violet of your mother's is. All the new blooms on a newly transplanted plant, a bit unusual don't you think? It's a sign for you from your mother. This is your blooming and flourishing time.

Don't give cancer another thought. Your Initiation is complete except for a few odds and ends like the port removal. You are now free at a profound level. You are gaining respect and trust in your inner knowing. It can't be short-circuited so easily now.

Did you see the Great Blue Heron just wing by? So close, so very close to you and your porch? (I look up the meaning in J.E. Cirlot's Dictionary of Symbols. "The heron is an ancient Egyptian symbol of the morning and of the generation of life. It carries favorable significance.")

Stay present! I send you messages all the time, messages declaring my Jove, affirmation, guidance, and some just for fun to see if you're alert!

Do you notice how at peace you are since you made your decision to stop "mainline" treatments and stay with your new health support program? That and happiness are your healing strategies now! Jelly side up! Count on me as I count on you!

Star-Thrower